CHANGE FOR A PENNY

A Small-Town, Workplace, Sweet
& Clean Romance

Kel Summers

Copyright © 2024 Kel Summers

Change for a Penny (On Air Book 1) is a work of fiction.

Copyright © 2024 Kel Summers All rights reserved

The characters and events portrayed in this book are fictitious. Any similarity to real persons, living or dead, is coincidental and not intended by the author.

No part of this book may be reproduced, or stored in a retrieval system, or transmitted in any form or by any means, electronic, mechanical, photocopying, recording, or otherwise, without express written permission of the publisher.

For permission requests, contact Kel Summers at hello@KelSummers.com.

Cover design by Kel Summers using resources from Canva Pro and/ or Microsoft Bing Image Creator from Designer and/or DALL-E.

Contents

Title Page
Copyright
Free Gift
Special Invitation
Chapter One — 1
Chapter Two — 17
Chapter Three — 25
Chapter Four — 37
Chapter Five — 47
Chapter Six — 57
Chapter Seven — 67
Chapter Eight — 77
Chapter Nine — 83
Chapter Ten — 89
Review This Book — 103
About Kel Summers — 105

Free Gift

For updates, sneak peeks, release dates, news, and more, sign up to receive Kel Summers newsletter and receive your FREE copy of Silent Sunsets or Summer in Carmel.

Visit the following website for Silent Sunsets: https://dl.bookfunnel.com/524b0dobl3

Visit the following website for Summer in Carmel: https://dl.bookfunnel.com/7rmrwfgzr6

Special Invitation

Join Kel Summers VIP Beach Retreat Romance Book Club and be the first to know about new releases, updates, and secret giveaways

https://www.facebook.com/groups/1294702547799834

Follow Kel Summers on Facebook

https://www.facebook.com/KelSummersRomanceAuthor/

Follow Kel Summers on Amazon and get notified of upcoming new releases

https://www.amazon.com/stores/Kel-Summers/author/B0C74QG5L7

Follow Kel Summers on BookBub

https://www.bookbub.com/authors/kel-summers

Follow Kel Summers on GoodReads.

https://www.goodreads.com/author/show/39592277.Kel_Summers

CHAPTER ONE

Penny's stomach twisted into knots as she approached the nondescript red-brick building. The heavy, gray clouds above seemed to mirror her mood, hanging low and oppressive, casting long shadows across the lot. She parked her Jeep but didn't move, gripping the steering wheel like it was the only thing anchoring her in place.

The Novack Family Services office wasn't much to look at from the outside—plain brick, a few windows, and a steel door that screamed "keep out." Yet, it wasn't the appearance that made her hesitate. It was the suffocating feeling of dread that coiled in her chest every time she pulled up here.

Taking a deep breath, she reached for the door handle. The cold steel pressed against her palm, slick from sweat, and for a brief moment, she considered turning around, jumping back into her Jeep, and driving away. Far away. Somewhere Jason Feeney couldn't haunt her, where broken dreams didn't linger in the sterile cubicle she was about to return to.

No. She pushed the door open instead. The dull creak echoed, swallowed by the buzz of fluorescent lights inside. She squared her shoulders, forcing herself to stand a little taller, even if her insides were trembling.

Penny Taylor, Case Manager for at-risk teens. She grimaced as the thought passed through her mind. It was a title she had once worn with pride. Now, it felt like a sentence, like shackles she couldn't break free from. Not hate exactly—hate was too strong, too final. Dislike, she corrected herself. Intense dislike.

With a slow exhale, she pulled herself into the lobby, glancing at the clock ticking on the far wall. 8:55 AM. It mocked her with its slow, deliberate movement. Five more minutes before she was officially on the clock.

You can get through this day, just like all the others, she told herself, though the reassurance felt hollow. Her stomach flipped again, and her mind spiraled, drawing up memories of the young, passionate woman she used to be. The one who believed she could make a difference, who wanted to change the world one troubled teen at a time. That woman had long since withered beneath the weight of bureaucracy and a broken system. Now, it just felt like she was slowly dying inside.

Dramatic much! She silently scolded herself.

"Okay, okay, three positives," she muttered under her breath, obeying her self-imposed rule to find the good when her thoughts turned bleak. "I earn a good salary. I love the kids I work with. I have great coworkers." She ticked them off on her fingers, mechanically, as she made her way to the office floor.

But the unspoken question remained: *Is that enough?*

As she crossed the threshold into the maze of cubicles, the familiar hum of chatter and keyboards greeted her. A few heads popped up from behind partitions, greeting her with half-hearted waves or nods. But all Penny saw was the worn, beige walls, and the lifeless fluorescent lights buzzing overhead, casting everything in a washed-out glow. The scent of burnt coffee lingered, a stark contrast to the tantalizing aroma from Talbot's Bakery, the one small joy on her otherwise dreadful commute.

"Morning, Penny!" A voice called out, too chipper for her current mood.

She forced a smile. "Morning," she replied automatically, her eyes scanning the room for a familiar face.

Sliding into her chair, she fired up her computer. The screen flickered to life, the hum of the fan accompanying the distant buzz of conversations from nearby desks. Her fingers hovered over the keyboard, but her mind wandered back to Jason Feeney—the root cause of her dissatisfaction, or so she told herself. *Jason Feeney.* Her ex. Even now, his name soured her mood, his dismissive words echoing in her head like the ghost of every shattered dream.

"You'll thank me later," he had said, sounding so sure of himself, so condescending. Penny could still see the smug twist of his lips as he dismissed her passion with a wave of his hand. *The newspaper industry is dying. Writing a best-selling novel is unrealistic.*

"*I can't keep doing this,*" she muttered under her breath, hating how his voice, even after all these years, still lived rent-free in her mind.

"Did you say something?"

Penny snapped back to reality, her heart skipping a beat. Stacie, her best friend, popped up beside her desk, blonde ponytail bouncing with every movement. "Did you have a rough weekend?" Stacie asked, concern lacing her otherwise cheerful tone.

"No, nothing like that. It's just... Well, it's just Monday," Penny shrugged, trying to sound nonchalant. She didn't want to admit how bad it had been. How bad it still was.

Stacie flashed a grin, her eyes dancing. "Well, Dan and I went hiking. You should've seen the views! I swear, it was like something out of a postcard. I can't wait to show you the pictures!"

Penny smiled, the kind you give when you don't have the energy to match someone's enthusiasm but don't want to bring them down either. "Sounds amazing. I can't wait to see them."

Before Stacie could launch into a full recap of the weekend, Mark, their fellow friend and co-worker, practically slid into Penny's cubicle. His eyes were wide with excitement—or maybe concern. It was hard to tell with Mark, who always had a flair for the dramatic.

"Did you guys see the email?" His voice dropped to a whisper, as if he was sharing state secrets.

"I just sat down. Mark. I haven't even been to the breakroom for coffee yet. And you know I never check my emails until I'm fully set up with coffee in hand." Penny replied, her voice laced with dry humor.

"Well, you might want to divert from your usual routine this morning because something's up," Mark lowered his voice even more. "A bunch of the corporate *bigwigs* are here, and we're having an all-team meeting in thirty minutes."

"You need to check your email. Now."

Penny raised an eyebrow and exchanged a look with Stacie before turning back to her screen, the knot in her stomach tightening as she clicked open the message.

> *The executive team will be addressing all Case Managers and support staff in the large conference room at 9:30 am sharp. Don't be late.*
>
> *Respectfully,*
> *Edward Kline.*

The email was short. Too short. No explanation, no context. Just a vague directive, which in Penny's experience was rarely a good sign. Her heart thudded against her ribs.

Stacie's chair squeaked first as she stood and leaned over the cubicle wall. Peering down at them, her expression was a mix of curiosity and concern. "What do you think that means?" she whispered, her voice now tinged with worry.

Penny's mind spiraled as a thousand scenarios danced through her thoughts, each one more absurd than the last. *Could they all be getting fired?* The idea lodged itself like a splinter, and for a split second, she allowed herself to indulge in the fantasy— a severance package so generous it would cushion her fall straight into a full-time writing career. She pictured herself at a cozy desk, sunlight streaming in through the window as she typed out her debut novel, a steaming cup of coffee at her side. No more cubicles, no more case files, just her words spilling onto the page.

She snapped back to reality, forcing the dream to dissolve like smoke. *That's not happening.* Instead, she glanced at Mark and Stacie, who were engaged in their usual back-and-forth like a verbal tennis match. She was caught in the middle, eyes flicking between them as they volleyed wild theories.

"Maybe they're finally giving us a raise," she threw out halfheartedly, her voice filled with forced optimism. But the second the words left her lips, she knew no one believed it. Not even her. The corner of Stacie's mouth twitched in what might have been a smile, but her eyes were far from convinced. Mark, wide-eyed and as dramatic as ever, didn't even entertain the thought.

Mark leaned forward, his voice dropping conspiratorially. "Did Dan mention anything?" His eyes darted over to Stacie like he expected her boyfriend to be privy to corporate secrets.

Stacie shook her head, blonde strands falling loose from her ponytail. "Nope. We don't talk about work on weekends," she replied, her tone suggesting it was a firm rule. "Besides, Dan doesn't have much to do with our division. You know how it is. The therapists and case managers might as well work in different universes."

Penny nodded in agreement. It was true. The therapists were the "Elite Team," as they liked to call themselves. Separate meetings, separate responsibilities. They shared the same building, but the overlap ended there. It wasn't an intentional divide, but it was one that everyone felt.

Mark, undeterred, leaned even closer over the cubicle wall, eyes glinting with excitement. "Okay, how about this? Maybe Mr. Novack embezzled all the money and ran off to Buenos Aires with his much younger assistant."

Stacie rolled her eyes, but a small laugh escaped her. "Oh please, Mark. Why Buenos Aires?"

Mark shrugged, the mischievous grin never leaving his face. "It's exotic. Dramatic. And you just know he'd have a younger assistant. Maybe she was in on it from the start. They probably had this whole scheme planned."

"Or," Penny added with mock seriousness, "maybe the accountant hasn't paid taxes in years, and the IRS is about to audit the place."

Mark clapped his hands together. "Yes! Exactly! Or it's a front for money laundering, and the FBI's gonna burst in any second!"

Wide-eyed, Mark popped his head up above the cubicle wall, scanning the office like he actually expected agents in dark suits to come marching through the door at any moment. His antics drew a stifled laugh from Penny, despite the tension gnawing at her insides.

Penny shook her head, trying to dismiss the anxiety creeping into her chest. "Mark, you seriously need to stop watching so many crime dramas." But the truth was, she couldn't shake the unease either. The higher-ups never mingled with the staff, and Mark—dramatics aside—usually had a sharp sense for when something was off. And something definitely felt off.

Stacie came around the partition, joining them in Penny's cubicle. Her eyes were wide with sudden realization. "You don't think someone died, do you?"

The question hit Penny like a cold splash of water. She blinked at Stacie, momentarily stunned by the shift in tone. "Let's not jump to conclusions," she said, though her pulse quickened. She forced a smile that felt tight and unnatural on her face. "Maybe it's just some new policy change or something boring."

"Yeah, maybe," Stacie murmured, though the look in her eyes said she wasn't entirely convinced.

Mark shrugged, leaning back in his chair, the conspiracies seemingly forgotten as he redirected the conversation. "Anyway, Penny, your column this weekend was spot on. I loved the part about the dating apps working together to keep 'the one' as far away as possible. Classic."

Penny blinked, momentarily thrown by the whiplash of topics. "Oh, thanks," she managed with a small smile, grateful for the shift away from their impending doom. "I figured you'd appreciate that theory."

"Appreciate it? I'm living it!" Mark threw his hands up dramatically. "I swear, every time I think I've found someone decent, they either ghost me or turn out to be an alien."

Stacie snorted. "An alien?"

"Okay, not literally an alien," Mark clarified with a wave of his hand. "But you get the idea. Penny's column nailed it. It's like all the good ones are just out of reach."

"Well," Penny said, leaning back in her chair, "maybe they're hiding in Buenos Aires with Mr. Novack and his assistant."

Mark burst out laughing, while Stacie shook her head, though she couldn't suppress her grin.

For a moment, the tension in the air lifted, replaced by the comfortable banter that usually filled their mornings. But it wasn't long before the uneasy quiet of the office returned, the impending meeting looming over them like the same dark cloud that had been following Penny all morning.

Penny glanced at the clock again. *9:20 AM.* Only ten minutes before they'd be called into the conference room. The knot in her stomach tightened once more, her earlier fantasy of severance packages and writing full-time now feeling more like a distant dream. Whatever was coming, it wasn't going to be good. She could feel it.

"Guess we'll find out soon enough," Mark murmured, his voice a low hum beneath the steady drone of the office. Penny nodded, but the weight of uncertainty still hung between them like a thick fog. Her gaze flicked to Stacie, who was chewing on her lower lip, a habit she had when she was nervous.

The clatter of keyboards and soft murmurs from surrounding cubicles filled the silence. Even the fluorescent lights seemed louder today, buzzing overhead with a dissonant hum that matched Penny's internal unease.

"Hey, aren't you meeting with the editor of the paper this week?" Stacie whispered as she leaned in closer so no one in the surrounding cubicles could hear.

Penny felt a flicker of excitement, the thought of the upcoming meeting sparking hope amidst the gloom. She straightened a little in her chair, as if the reminder of her dreams gave her a brief surge of energy. "Yeah, Thursday. I've got my portfolio all set, and I've been rehearsing what I want to say. I'm nervous as hell, though." Her fingers tapped lightly on her desk as she spoke, betraying the tension beneath her calm tone. "I guess the worst that could happen is that he'll say no, right?"

Stacie nodded, her eyes warm with encouragement. "But that's not going to happen. You've got this, Penny."

Mark suddenly pumped his fist in the air. "I'm rooting for you, too! I mean, I don't want to lose you here, but I know this isn't where your heart is." His voice softened, his usual theatrics giving way to sincerity. "Your kids, though… they're gonna miss you like crazy."

Penny's chest tightened at the mention of her kids. The teens she worked with were a mixed bag—some were troubled, some just needed a little extra guidance, and some tugged at her heartstrings more than she cared to admit. "Yeah, I wonder how they'll split up my caseload if I go. You know who I'd give to you in a heartbeat," Penny said, turning to Stacie with a knowing grin.

Stacie grinned back. "Oh, I know! You've got a couple of girls

I'd take on in an instant." Her expression softened. "I just can't get through to the boys the same way you can. I swear, you've got a magic touch with them."

Penny chuckled, but there was a truth behind Stacie's words. The boys were tougher to reach, but somehow, she had found ways to connect with them. Maybe it was because she never gave up, or maybe it was because she saw pieces of herself in their struggles. Either way, she knew letting them go would be hard. "You do great with the girls, though. Some of my boys... yeah, they're a challenge."

Mark, who had been quiet for a moment, let out a soft groan, stretching his arms above his head. "I didn't even think about that. I already have more cases than the rest of you, and if they dump more on me... Ugh! I swear, some of these kids are just determined to end up in juvie, no matter what I do."

Penny nodded sympathetically. The burden they carried as case managers was heavy, and it didn't always have a happy ending. Despite their best efforts, despite pouring their hearts into these kids, there were times when the system—or life itself—seemed stacked against them. "It's not easy, Mark. But we do what we can, right?"

Mark's eyes darkened, the weight of his caseload etched across his features. "Yeah, but sometimes it feels like we're just patching up holes in a sinking ship. Some of these kids... they've got so much working against them."

Penny's heart ached at the truth in his words. It was one of the hardest parts of the job—knowing that no matter how hard they tried, some kids might still fall through the cracks. She had long since learned how to compartmentalize, but some days, it was impossible to leave the job at the office. It crept into her thoughts during dinner, tugged at her as she tried to sleep, and haunted her in quiet moments.

Stacie, sensing the heaviness settling over them, offered a weak smile. "Hey, we do our best. That's all we can do, right? And if Penny gets this job at the paper, we'll just have to figure out how to manage without her magic."

Penny smiled, grateful for the attempt to lighten the mood. But before she could respond, Mark glanced at the clock and then subtly tilted his chin toward the hallway. "I think it's time," he said, his voice dropping low.

Penny watched as people around her began to rise from their desks, the soft scrape of chairs echoing through the office. The air felt different, heavier, as if everyone was holding their breath. She reached for her notepad and her favorite pen, the one with the smooth ink flow that helped her feel more in control, though her grip was tighter than usual.

"Here goes nothing," she muttered under her breath, forcing a lightness into her voice that she didn't quite feel. Her mind wandered to her lunch, or rather, the lunch she'd forgotten on the counter in her rush to get out the door. "By the way, do you two want to grab lunch today? I realized halfway here that I left mine sitting right next to my coffee maker."

Mark bobbed his head, already gathering his things as they prepared to head to the conference room. "Yes, but please, no soup or salad joint today. I have a feeling whatever they're about to tell us, I'm gonna need something with more... substance."

Penny chuckled softly, appreciating his attempt at humor, but the tension swirling in her chest refused to loosen. Before Stacie could respond, the hum of conversation around them fell abruptly silent. Penny followed the collective gaze of the room to the front, where Mr. Kline, the Operations Director, had stepped forward.

"Thank you for being here," Mr. Kline's voice boomed across the room, calm but devoid of warmth.

Mark leaned over, whispering just loud enough for Penny to hear. "Like we had a choice," he muttered, his sarcasm eliciting a stifled laugh from her as she nudged him with her shoulder.

Penny shifted in her seat, trying to focus on Mr. Kline's words, but the steady stream of company jargon about policy changes and deadlines quickly blurred into the background. Her mind began to drift.

Why couldn't this just be an email? Penny wondered, tapping her pen absently against her notepad. She sketched lazy circles in the margin, her thoughts growing more detached from the present until a sudden throat-clearing from the front of the room brought her back.

The atmosphere shifted. A low murmur rippled through the crowd, an electric charge of anticipation and dread. Penny looked up to see Mr. Novak, the company's founder, enter the room. His presence alone seemed to command attention, even from those who had been half asleep during Mr. Kline's droning.

This must be the "top brass" Mark was talking about. Penny straightened in her chair, feeling the tension ratchet up a notch as Mr. Novak moved to the front of the room, his expression cool and unreadable.

There was no greeting, no easing into the announcement. Mr. Novak wasted no time on pleasantries. His voice was clipped, businesslike. "I'll keep this short so you can all get back to work," he began, his gaze sweeping the room with an almost predatory sharpness. "Due to some changes in our company's vision for the future, we will be restructuring how we do business."

The word *restructuring* dropped into the room like a grenade. Penny felt the knot in her stomach tighten, her pulse quickening as Mr. Novak continued.

"Over the next week, a team of executives will meet with each of you to discuss the vision and the restructuring and how it will affect you and your pod. Pods A through C will be addressed today. Please return to your desks and wait to be called."

Penny heard a rustle of movement, someone in the back raising a hand, but Mr. Novak's icy stare silenced them before they could speak. "There will be plenty of time for questions when you meet with the executive team," he added abruptly, his tone making it clear there would be no questions now. Then, with a curt nod, he turned and walked out of the room, leaving a stunned silence in his wake.

Penny exchanged a glance with Mark and Stacie, both of whom looked as uneasy as she felt. "Well, that didn't sound good," she whispered, her voice barely audible over the buzz of nervous whispers that had erupted around them.

"Restructuring?" Mark's voice was a low rumble of disbelief. "That sounds like corporate speak for 'you're fired.'"

Penny bit her lip, feeling a cold sweat trickle down her spine. She'd joked before about losing her job, how a severance package would be her golden ticket to finally pursue writing full-time. But now, the reality of it felt different. Without a solid Plan B, the idea of losing her job filled her with a creeping dread. *What if they really do let us go?*

Stacie, always the worrier, was twisting the rings on her fingers—an old nervous habit Penny recognized all too well. The look in Stacie's eyes mirrored Penny's own uncertainty. The joke about losing their jobs didn't seem so funny now.

Mark leaned in as they made their way back to their desks. "Do you think we can add alcohol to our lunch?" he whispered, his voice a mix of dry humor and genuine anxiety.

Penny forced a smile and nodded, though her mind was racing. *Would they even make it to lunch?* They were Pod C, and from the way Mr. Kline and the unfamiliar man in a sharp suit were striding toward them, she had a sinking feeling that their time was up sooner than expected.

The man—someone Penny didn't recognize—smiled at them, though it wasn't a warm smile. It was the kind of smile that made Penny think of crocodiles eyeing its lunch. "Pod C, would you please collect your files and bring them to the small conference room?" His tone was polite but firm, the kind of tone that left no room for argument.

Penny exchanged a glance with Mark and Stacie, their eyes wide with shared apprehension. They grabbed their case files in silence, the weight of the unknown pressing down on them like a lead blanket. As they walked toward the small conference room, Penny didn't have to turn around to know that all eyes in the office were on them.

CHAPTER TWO

"This is karma, you know?" Penny said to the reflection in the bathroom mirror. Her face was pale, her eyes swollen from hours of crying. "The universe is giving you exactly what you asked for." She leaned closer to the glass, studying the woman staring back at her. She barely recognized herself.

She'd been in her pajamas since late Monday morning, ever since the moment she had been escorted out of Novack Family Services with a cardboard box of her belongings balanced awkwardly in her arms. The memory of wide-eyed stares, the whispers behind cupped hands, and the palpable relief from her colleagues that it wasn't them still lingered in her mind, making her stomach twist with renewed nausea.

Mark and Stacie had both come by, their voices full of forced cheer, trying to lift her spirits. They had brought coffee and pastries, like sugary comfort could somehow fill the gaping void in her chest. Their motivational speeches had bounced off her like rubber bullets. She appreciated their efforts, sure, but there was no shaking the numbness that had settled deep inside her. She remained rooted in her pajamas, tissues always within reach, staring listlessly at the TV and ignoring the world outside.

"Three months' pay and a glowing recommendation," she muttered, shaking her head. It was more than she had expected, but it wouldn't last forever. She'd been given a soft landing, but the ground beneath it was still fragile.

The faint tick of the clock in the hallway signaled that her self-imposed pity party was nearing its end. She told herself that she could have forty-eight hours of wallowing, and in just a few short hours her time would be up. Tomorrow, she had a meeting with Tom Greely, the editor-in-chief of *The County Star*. What had once been a casual request for an additional day for her column had morphed into something much more urgent. It was now a desperate plea for full-time work.

Penny sighed, her eyes scanning the cluttered living room beyond the bathroom door. Half-empty coffee mugs littered the coffee table, discarded notebooks lay scattered on the floor, and an overwhelming sense of disarray clung to the space. "This place is a disaster," she said to herself. "But first things first. I need a shower."

The hot water worked its magic, the steam curling around her, loosening the knot of anxiety in her chest. As she scrubbed her skin with her favorite citrus-scented body wash, she felt the grime of despair wash away. It wasn't a miracle cure, but it helped. It was a small step toward feeling like herself again.

When she finally stepped out, she wrapped a wrapped around her then sat on the edge of her bed and pulled out a fresh notebook. The clean, unmarked pages seemed to mock her, but she brushed it off. She needed to face reality. No more running from it. Her finances needed sorting. She had no savings to fall back on, having always thought she would start a savings account "one day." She'd never put herself on a budget either.

"Better late than never, Penny." Her grandmother's voice echoed in her mind, reminding her of the lessons she'd passed down:

For the next hour, Penny painstakingly crafted a modest financial plan. She scribbled down numbers, calculating her car payment and insurance, groceries, utilities—everything she could think of—and the salary she'd need to survive. The simple act of writing it out gave her a strange sense of control. It was like she was rejoining the land of the living, even if the plan did seem a little fragile.

When the budget was done, she updated her resume and scrolled through the job boards, hoping for something promising. Three months of severance was a blessing, but it would run out fast. The one saving grace? She didn't have to worry about rent. Her gran had left her the house, the cozy sanctuary Penny had spent countless childhood summers in.

She smiled, glancing around the living room. It still held her gran's touch—plush armchairs, soft throws, the scent of lavender still faint in the air. Living here made her feel close to her again. Her heart warmed, thinking about her gran's wisdom and quirky beliefs in energy and manifestation, the nights they'd spent talking about the universe and its mysterious ways. Penny missed her more than she could put into words, but the house held her memories like a gentle embrace.

After tidying up a bit, Penny cracked open her laptop. Her fingers hovered over the keys for a moment before she began typing up next week's column. The familiar rhythm of her typing was comforting, like a heartbeat steadying her thoughts. But as soon as she finished, a nagging thought tugged at her. Should she write something more? Something... explosive? The idea of penning an exposé on the broken social services system flashed through her mind. She could imagine it now—a scathing piece that would lay bare the dysfunction she'd witnessed every day at Novack Family Services.

But the urge passed quickly as she thought better of it. Penny wasn't ready to burn bridges. Not yet, anyway. "Maybe one day," she whispered, shaking her head.

A sudden knock at the door jolted her from her thoughts, causing her to nearly spill her glass of sweet tea all over her laptop. Her breath caught in her throat. "Now, wouldn't that just be the icing on the cake?"

"Penny, are you in there?" Stacie's voice drifted through the door.

Penny glanced at the clock, surprised at how quickly the day had passed. Stacie had arrived on time, as she often did, despite the increased workload since Penny's departure. During the layoffs, each pod had lost a member, and Penny's kids had been split between Mark and Stacie. The thought of her kids still tugged at her, but knowing they were in good hands helped ease the ache.

"I'm here, hold on," Penny called, padding across the room to open the door. The instant she did, the smell of garlic and parmesan hit her, and her stomach growled in response.

"Wings!" Penny grinned, grabbing one of the bags from Stacie. "I hope you brought extra, because I'm starving."

"I wouldn't leave you hanging," Stacie replied with a laugh, carrying the food to the coffee table. "And yes, I even got you a salad."

Penny beamed as she grabbed a couple of beers from the fridge. "I knew you were my favorite for a reason."

"So, what's the vibe at the office?" Penny asked, plopping down on the couch.

Stacie cracked open a container and sighed. "Work's been… tense. Everyone's walking on eggshells, hoping the execs don't come back for another round of layoffs."

"You think that's possible?" Penny asked, suddenly worried for her friends.

"I don't know. Dan says the therapists haven't been touched yet, so maybe they're next." She shrugged, biting into a wing. "But he doesn't seem worried. Oh, and—big news—we're thinking of moving in together."

"Wait, what?" Penny's eyes widened, a genuine smile spreading across her face. "That's huge! Why didn't you lead with that?"

"I figured food was more important to you right now," Stacie teased, brushing her hands on a napkin. "But yeah, it feels right."

Penny nodded, taking a sip of her beer. "That's amazing,

Stacie. Dan seems like a great guy. But I don't know if I could have a therapist for a boyfriend. I'd be too worried that he was diagnosing everything I did, from how I folded my clothes to how many times I checked the door locks every night."

Stacie cocked her head playfully. "Exactly how many times do you check the door every night?"

Penny laughed. "Don't judge. I live alone! It's called being cautious."

Stacie laughed and opened a wet wipe to clean her fingers before reaching for her beer. "How are you feeling about tomorrow?"

"Good, I think. I have my portfolio ready, and the stats show my column is popular. I also put out some other feelers today. You know, just in case working full-time at the paper doesn't work out. I mean, the situation isn't ideal, but I'm doing much better than I was."

They settled into comfortable conversation, their laughter filling the room, easing the tension that had hung over Penny since Monday. As they ate, Stacie suddenly leaned forward, eyes gleaming. "You know, I was thinking. I know you're set on writing, but have you ever considered doing a podcast?" Stacie asked. "You could probably do both. I think people would tune in to hear your original stories. I mean, it's not much different than an audiobook. Or, better yet," Stacie leaned forward, excitement bubbling in her voice. "You could take your Dating Dilemmas column and turn that into a podcast. People could call in and share their horrible date stories. Oh! I'm loving this idea."

Penny's eyes lit up. "You know, that's actually a great idea. I've never thought about it that way."

"Think about it, Penny. You've got the voice for it, and your stories are already so engaging. Why not give it a shot?"

Penny's eyes lit up as the idea began to take shape in her mind. "Dating Disasters," she mused, excitement building. "Or maybe... Matchmaking Misadventures."

Stacie laughed, clapping her hands. "Yes! And you could have a segment called *Flirty Fails* where people share their most embarrassing dating moments."

Penny's mind raced with possibilities. "I could give advice too. I mean, I've had more than enough bad dates to know what not to do."

Stacie grinned, her excitement infectious. "Exactly! You could even have relationship experts on as guests. And think of all the stories you already have from your column. You could get it up and running in no time."

For the first time in days, Penny felt a spark of something new—a sense of purpose. "This... this could really work," she said softly, leaning back against the couch. "I love the idea, Stace. It's like everything I enjoy—writing, storytelling, and helping people—wrapped into one."

Stacie reached over and squeezed her hand. "I'm telling you, it's the perfect next step for you. And I'll be your number one listener."

Penny laughed, but her heart felt lighter. As they continued brainstorming, ideas flying between them, the weight that had been pressing down on her for days began to lift. She wasn't out of the woods yet, but for the first time in a long time, she could see a path forward. A new chapter was beginning to take shape.

"I really needed this. I feel like I finally have something to look forward to." Penny said suddenly, her voice soft and filled with gratitude.

Stacie smiled and squeezed Penny's arm. "I think this is the kick you needed to follow your dreams. I just hate that it all happened this way. Call me as soon as you know something, okay?"

Her voice caught in her throat that was tight with emotion, "I will, Stacie. Thanks for everything—the food, the support, all of it."

They hugged tightly, and Penny felt a surge of gratitude for her friend's unwavering positivity. As Stacie left, Penny stood in the doorway for a moment, soaking in the quiet of her house. She looked around the living room, the comforting clutter of her collections mingling with her gran's treasured items, and she couldn't help but feel that everything was happening exactly as it was supposed to happen.

CHAPTER THREE

The next morning, golden sunlight streamed through the window, casting warm, hopeful rays across Penny's bedroom. The gentle warmth against her skin was like a quiet invitation to step into a new beginning. She stretched, arms reaching toward the ceiling, and felt a tiny spark of excitement ripple through her. Today was the day.

She flung the covers aside and padded across the room, her feet sinking into the plush carpet. The familiar hum of the house greeted her, but the usual heavy weight of uncertainty didn't follow her as she headed to the bathroom. She stepped into the shower, letting the hot water cascade over her, washing away the remnants of sleep and lingering doubts. With each drop, her nerves eased just a little more.

After drying off, she glanced at the outfit she had carefully laid out the night before. It was simple but sharp: a fitted blazer, a classic blouse, and tailored pants. Not too flashy, but professional enough to make a statement. This wasn't just another article pitch. This was her future. And she wanted Mr. Greely to take her seriously.

Penny had known Mr. Greely for years, ever since her part-time job writing sports summaries in high school. Back then, he had been the sports editor, the one who had given her her first byline. She still remembered the thrill of seeing her name in print, how proud she felt contributing to the paper. That seemed like a lifetime ago.

Now, dressed and ready, Penny grabbed her laptop bag and her lunch, leftovers from the night before. She took a deep breath at the front door, savoring the crisp morning air that greeted her as she stepped outside. It was the kind of cool breeze that carried a sense of renewal with it, sharp and invigorating. "You got this," she whispered, pushing aside the small tremor of anxiety that threatened to creep in. Then, to ground herself, she softly repeated her favorite mantra: "The universe is friendly and works in my favor."

The newspaper office was nestled in the heart of downtown, just a few blocks past the Novak building. She focused on her breathing as she drove, deliberately avoiding a glance at her old workplace. Instead, she let herself watch the world wake up—people walking their dogs, coffee shops bustling with the morning crowd, the comforting hum of small-town life continuing as always. But today, the world felt different. Penny was filled with hope, knowing she stood on the brink of something new.

Pulling into the newspaper's parking lot, she was relieved to find a spot near the front door. For a moment, she stayed in her Jeep, hands gripping the steering wheel as she reviewed her proposal one last time in her head. A buzz of nervous energy hummed beneath her skin. This was her shot, and she couldn't afford to let it slip away. *The County Star* wasn't just any paper—it was the largest in the county, and with rumors swirling about expanding into digital content, Penny wanted to be part of that future. The possibilities felt endless.

With one final glance in the rearview mirror, she gave herself a firm nod. "If somebody can do it, I can do it," she whispered fiercely before stepping out and making her way to the entrance.

Inside, she was greeted by the familiar face of Daphne, the paper's administrative assistant, who had known Penny all her life. Daphne beamed, approaching her with the warm familiarity only small towns offer.

"Penny, my dear, how are you?" Daphne asked, though Penny sensed the question was loaded with more than just polite curiosity. Word about her layoff had likely made its way through town by now—small towns had a way of spreading news faster than social media ever could.

"I'm well, thank you," Penny replied, flashing a polite smile, steering the conversation back to business. "I'm here to see Mr. Greely."

Daphne nodded. "He's running a bit late, but he asked me to set you up with a desk while you wait. Why don't you grab some coffee first?"

"Thanks, Daphne. I might just do that," Penny said, making her way toward the break room.

The smell of freshly brewed coffee wafted through the air,

and Penny let herself inhale deeply. The rich, familiar scent was like an old friend, steadying her nerves. As she poured herself a cup, the sound of the newsroom buzzed in the background—the click of keyboards, phones ringing, murmurs of conversations about the day's headlines. It was comforting, that hum of productivity, a rhythm Penny had missed.

Walking back toward the open floor, she spotted Bonnie, one of the more seasoned reporters, hunched over her desk, typing furiously. Bonnie had been a year ahead of Penny in high school and had worked at the paper ever since college. Despite the years, Bonnie hadn't changed much, she still had the same determined gleam in her eyes, chasing stories with an infectious enthusiasm.

"Penny, how are you?" Bonnie looked up, her smile warm as she paused her work. "Your column the other day was fantastic. I love your take on the dating scene—it makes me grateful I'm not part of it anymore," she added with a laugh.

"Thanks, Bonnie. I appreciate that," Penny replied, smiling despite the flurry of nerves in her stomach. "I'm hoping to join you guys full-time soon."

Bonnie's eyebrows shot up, her smile widening. "Really? That would be amazing. I always thought you'd end up here. What's the scoop?"

Penny shrugged lightly, trying to keep her tone casual. "I'm meeting with Mr. Greely today. Hoping he'll either add me to the staff or give me more articles to write. I've heard whispers about going digital, and I'd love to help with that."

"Oh, you've heard about that, too?" Bonnie leaned forward, lowering her voice conspiratorially. "His nephew has been working on it for a while now. But who knows—our readers are die-hard print fans. Not sure how it'll play out, but it's exciting."

Penny grinned. "It's like the debate between e-readers and print books. Some people just love the feel of paper."

Bonnie chuckled. "Exactly. Anyway, I hope you get it. You've always belonged here."

Before Penny could respond, she heard her name being called from across the room. Daphne waved her over, and Penny's heart skipped a beat.

"Mr. Greely's ready for you," Daphne said as Penny approached. "He figured you probably skipped breakfast, just like old times, so he had me grab you an egg salad sandwich. Still your favorite?"

Penny's heart warmed at the thoughtfulness. "He knows me too well," she said with a smile.

As she walked toward Mr. Greely's office, the familiar comfort of the newsroom buoyed her spirits. Stepping inside, she saw Mr. Greely standing by his desk, a sandwich and soda already set out for her.

"Penny! Still saving the world?" he greeted with his signature warm smile.

Penny unwrapped the sandwich and sighed, a wry smile tugging at her lips. "I was until Monday. Now I'm looking for a job."

"You're kidding me!" Mr. Greely exclaimed, his brow furrowing with concern. "I just heard a news report saying there are more kids than ever getting hooked on these drugs. What happened?"

"Cutbacks, I guess," Penny replied, frustration edging her voice. "I was told it was due to restructuring and downsizing, and I was promptly shown the door. Everyone's caseloads were out of control, so it doesn't make sense to me either. But here we are."

Mr. Greely leaned back in his chair, thoughtful. "Well, if that's the case, how about adding some hours here? One of our writers is on leave, and we could use your help. Plus, my nephew's digital initiative could use your insight."

Penny's heart soared. "I'd love that."

He laughed and took a sip of his drink. "I would love for you to come back. I'm in meetings the rest of the day and playing golf tomorrow. Can you come back on Monday? We'll sign the paperwork and discuss the salary then. It won't be life-changing money, but you should be able to buy the good bologna at least."

Penny laughed, relief flooding through her. "Sounds like a plan, thanks!"

They finished their sandwiches, chatting about their families. Mr. Greely and her dad golfed together a few times a month. Penny confided that she hadn't told her parents about the job situation yet. They were still on vacation and wouldn't be back until next week. He promised to keep her secret. Her mom would be thrilled since she always worried about Penny going into strangers' homes that weren't always in the best neighborhoods.

Crumpling up her sandwich wrapper, Penny stood to leave, feeling a weight lift off her shoulders. "Thank you again," she said, pausing at the door. "I'll see you on Monday."

Mr. Greely smiled warmly. "Looking forward to it, Penny."

Walking back to the desk she had been using, Penny felt a renewed sense of purpose. Things were finally starting to look up.

As soon as Penny slid into her car, she fumbled for her phone, her hands shaking with excitement. She quickly dialed Stacie's number, her heart pounding in her chest. The moment Stacie picked up, Penny blurted out the news, unable to contain herself.

"Stacie, I got the job!" she exclaimed, her voice trembling.

There was a brief pause, followed by cheers so loud that Penny had to hold the phone away from her ear.

"Woo-hoo! Way to go, Penny!" Stacie's voice was full of joy.

"You did it! This is amazing!" Mark chimed in. His enthusiasm was unmistakable as he clapped in the background.

Penny felt a rush of relief and ecstasy wash over her. She was finally on the path to living her dream. She pinched herself, ensuring she wasn't dreaming. The tingly excitement spread all the way to her toes, making her giggle. Things were finally turning around for her. And with a few free days off and a paycheck guaranteed, she decided to treat herself.

The mall was buzzing with life as Peny wandered through the stores. Each store she entered felt like a small victory, and each purchase was a small reminder that she was free to reinvent herself and to embrace this new chapter of her life. The weight of the past week lifted more and more with each purchase. The weight of the past week, the anxiety of losing her job, was slowly peeling away, layer by layer, with each swipe of her card.

In front of a full-length mirror, she held up a cream blouse, the soft silk flowing through her fingers. She imagined herself stepping confidently into the newspaper office, the gentle swish of her skirt following her every move. Penny smiled at her reflection, twirling a little, feeling her confidence build as she pictured herself not just fitting in but owning the space. The blouse, paired with a sleek pencil skirt and new heels, was her visual armor, and she needed every bit of it for the new challenges ahead.

"Yeah, this is it," she whispered to herself, turning from side to side, admiring the way the outfit made her feel—polished, prepared, and just a little bit fierce.

The day carried on like this, with Penny moving from store to store, her mood lifting with every purchase. By the time she finally emerged from the mall, her arms were heavy with bags, but her heart felt light. A sense of satisfaction settled deep within her. She needed this—retail therapy at its finest. But it wasn't just about the new clothes... it was more about finally claiming her future. As she loaded the bags into the Jeep, she felt a giddy rush of excitement.

On the way home from the mall she stopped and ordered

take-out from the little Italian restaurant downtown. The familiar and comforting smell of garlic and marinara sauce filled the air. "This day just keeps getting better and better," she laughed as her stomach growled loudly in anticipation of her upcoming feast. For the first time in a long time, everything felt right, and Penny wasn't worried about tomorrow.

Her phone buzzed just as she pulled into the driveway. She turned off the engine and grabbed it, she smiled when she saw it was a group text from Stacie and Mark. Penny unlocked the phone, her eyes skimming the message.

Happy hour tomorrow?

The message read, accompanied by a celebratory emoji.

Her smile turned into a wide grin as she quickly typed out a reply.

Absolutely! Count me in!

She added a celebratory gif for good measure, chuckling to herself before hopping out of the Jeep.

With her shopping bags clutched in one hand and the takeout balanced in the other, Penny made her way into the house, feeling lighter than she had in weeks. She paused in the doorway for a moment, just breathing in the quiet comfort of her home. It was a stark contrast to the chaos of the mall, but in its own way, just as satisfying. This was her space, her sanctuary.

In her bedroom, she tossed the bags onto the bed, the sound of the fabric rustling making her smile. She wouldn't unpack them just yet; the excitement of having something new to wear tomorrow was enough for now. Instead, she changed into her favorite pair of yoga pants and an oversized sweatshirt, the soft fabric hugging her like an old friend.

In the kitchen, she poured herself a glass of wine and settled onto the couch with her Italian feast, the rich, comforting scents filling the room. The lasagna was perfect—a balance of melted cheese and hearty sauce that made her mouth water as she dug in.

She turned on her favorite reality TV show, just in time to see the newest batch of bachelorettes stepping out of the long, dark limousine, each vying for their moment in the spotlight. Penny couldn't help but laugh at the drama unfolding on-screen, her own life suddenly feeling a lot less chaotic in comparison.

With a contented sigh, she took another bite of her lasagna and a sip of wine, feeling the tension from the past week melt away. The combination of good food, trashy TV, and new possibilities on the horizon made everything seem a little brighter. It was almost comical how much better she felt, knowing that just days ago, she had been spiraling.

She hadn't felt this good in so long, and as she sat there on her couch, wrapped in warmth and comfort, she realized something. Maybe losing her job hadn't been the catastrophe she'd feared. Maybe it had been the push she needed to chase her dreams.

Penny smiled to herself, taking another sip of wine, as the show played in the background. It was almost funny how things worked out sometimes—how cut-backs and setbacks could turn into new opportunities. She hadn't expected it at first, but maybe the universe really was working in her favor after all.

CHAPTER FOUR

The next night, Penny walked into their favorite happy hour spot, a cozy bar known for its nachos and pitchers of margaritas. The place was buzzing with chatter and laughter, and the familiar atmosphere immediately put her at ease. She had spent the day finishing her column and working on story ideas, researching past articles that were written by the journalist she was covering for. She was determined to be prepared and make the most of this opportunity.

As she scanned the room, she spotted Mark first. His figure bobbed and weaved between tables, hands raised high above his head in a dramatic display. "There she is! The next Pulitzer Prize winner!" he shouted, his voice booming over the chatter and causing heads to turn.

Penny's cheeks flushed with a mix of embarrassment and delight. She laughed, motioning for him to quiet down. "Oh, stop it!" she giggled, approaching the table where Stacie was standing, waving a sparkly tiara and a sash that read, "Princess Penny" in bold, glittery letters.

"You guys are too much!" Penny exclaimed, her eyes

sparkling with joy.

Stacie pulled her into a tight hug, her voice brimming with genuine pride. "I'm so stinking proud of you!"

The server arrived at their booth, and they quieted down just long enough to place their usual order. Nachos piled high with toppings and a pitcher of margaritas to share.

With a giggle, Penny picked up the tiara and placed it on her head, adjusting the sash around her shoulders. "Might as well wear it if you went to all the trouble," she teased, posing with a mock princess wave.

Mark smirked and raised his margarita glass. "A toast! To Princess Penny—may her reign at the paper be long and full of well-deserved Pulitzers!"

Penny rolled her eyes but clinked her glass against his, the gesture making her heart swell with love for her friends. They spent the next hour chatting animatedly, their conversation weaving in and out of playful banter and serious talk about the future. Penny found herself glancing around the bar occasionally, soaking in the cozy atmosphere and the buzzing energy of the night. There was something comforting about the place, with its worn wooden tables, twinkling string lights, and the low hum of music playing in the background.

Across the room, the karaoke stage was lit up with flashing lights, and brave souls took turns singing everything from classic rock to guilty-pleasure pop hits. Penny wasn't one to sing solo, but she had a fondness for encouraging her friends to take the plunge.

"Remember when Mark butchered *Bohemian Rhapsody*?" Penny asked, pointing to a middle-aged man on stage who was valiantly attempting the same song.

Stacie burst into laughter, her eyes crinkling at the memory. "Oh my God, yes! And he swore he nailed it."

"I did nail it," Mark chimed in, a grin plastered across his face. "The crowd loved me."

"They loved you, all right," Penny teased, her laughter bubbling up. "Loved watching you leave the stage."

Stacie's eyes sparkled with mischief as she turned to Penny, her hand outstretched. "C'mon, Penny! It's our turn!" she said, her voice bubbling with excitement.

In the next instant Penny found herself being dragged onto the stage for a duet. Their voices blended together as they sang off-key but with genuine enthusiasm. The crowd clapped along, and Penny couldn't help but laugh as her earlier reservations melted away in the infectious enthusiasm of the moment.

Back at the table, breathless and buzzing with energy, Penny took a sip of her margarita, letting the happiness of the night sink in. She glanced around, feeling the warmth of her friends, the hum of the bar, and the promise of the new chapter that awaited her. Everything felt right—finally.

Suddenly, there was a soft gasp from Stacie, and Mark leaned in, whispering loud enough for anyone nearby to hear, "Don't look now, but that guy over there has been watching you all night."

Penny's heart skipped a beat. "Where?" she asked, her curiosity immediately piqued.

Mark nodded subtly in the direction of a man sitting a few tables over. Penny's eyes followed, and when they landed on him, she noticed that he didn't look away. Their gazes locked for a moment, and Penny felt a shy smile tug at her lips. He was handsome, with dark wavy hair and horn-rimmed glasses—he reminded her of a young Dean Cain, the kind of guy who could make the heart race without even trying.

"Oh, he's cute," Stacie whispered, her excitement barely contained.

"You should go talk to him," Mark added, giving her a playful nudge.

Penny hesitated, her heart fluttering with nerves. Her track record with men wasn't stellar. Between her ex, who had sent her life careening off course, and two fleeting relationships that hadn't lasted more than a few months, she wasn't exactly brimming with confidence. Mark always teased her for being too picky, while Stacie was more about taking risks, throwing caution to the wind.

Penny glanced at the mystery man again, her mind racing. Maybe tonight was different. Maybe this was her chance to step out of her comfort zone and see where it led. With a burst of bravery, she tipped her glass towards him and flashed her most confident smile.

The man's eyes sparkled with amusement, and his friendly smile broadened. Penny's heart skipped a beat. *Why not?* she thought, her pulse quickening.

Stacie nudged her again. "Go on, Penny. What do you have to lose?"

Taking a deep breath, Penny stood up and smoothed down her dress, trying to exude confidence she didn't quite feel. "Okay, I'm doing it," she whispered to herself, her heart pounding in her chest as she walked toward him.

As she approached, the noise of the bar seemed to blur into the background. Her focus narrowed to the man sitting across the room, his gaze never wavering as she neared. When she finally stood in front of him, her voice came out softer than she intended, "Hi, I'm Penny."

The man's warm smile widened. "Hi, Penny. I'm Nathan. Care to join me?"

Penny glanced back at her table, where Stacie and Mark were watching with barely contained excitement. She smiled, feeling a rush of boldness. "Actually, I was wondering if you'd like to join us?"

Nathan looked toward her friends, then back at her, his smile never fading. "Sure, Lead the way."

Penny led him back to their table, her friends grinning like Cheshire cats. "Everyone, this is Nathan," she introduced. "Nathan, these are my friends, Stacie and Mark."

"Nice to meet you," Nathan said, shaking their hands.

The moment they sat down, Stacie leaned forward, her eyes

twinkling with curiosity.

"So, Nathan, where are you from?" Stacie asked the moment he sat down. Her tone was friendly, but she was clearly fishing for information.

Penny shot Stacie a warning look. She knew her friend was just looking out for her, but she half expected Stacie's next words to be, "And what are your intentions with *our little Penny*?" But Nathan didn't seem to mind. He leaned closer so they could hear him over the karaoke that began to blare from the stage.

Nathan smiled easily, as if he'd expected the inquisition. "I'm originally from the West Coast—Washington, but I've been here a few months. My family has a business in town, and I'm here helping out with a project."

Mark raised an eyebrow, intrigued. "What kind of project? Something top-secret? Like an *'I could tell you but then I'd have to kill you'* type of project?"

Nathan chuckled. "Nothing as serious as that, I promise. It's a family business, so I've been helping with some of the tech stuff. You know, modernizing systems, streamlining operations. The glamorous life of IT work."

"Ah, IT," Stacie chimed in, nodding knowingly. "So, you're the guy who everyone calls when their computer won't turn on, huh?"

Nathan grinned. "Pretty much. I've got the whole 'have you tried turning it off and on again?' routine down to a science."

Penny, feeling more relaxed now that her friends seemed to

like him, smiled. "And you studied that in school, right?"

"Yeah," Nathan replied, turning to Penny. "I double-majored in IT and business. Thought it'd give me options, and it definitely keeps me busy."

Mark leaned back in his chair, crossing his arms with a playful smirk. "So, is this family project going to keep you here for good? Or are you just passing through?"

Nathan paused, considering his answer. "I haven't decided yet. I really like it here—small town life, the people, the pace. It's different from Seattle, but in a good way. So, I don't know... I guess we'll see what happens."

Stacie, clearly approving, exchanged a quick glance with Penny before grinning. "Well, if you stick around, you've got good company. Penny knows all the best spots."

Nathan shot Penny a warm smile. "I'm counting on it."

Penny blushed, but she couldn't help smiling back, her earlier nerves were now completely forgotten.

As the night wore on, the conversation flowed effortlessly, laughter bubbling up from their table as if they'd all known each other for years. Penny found herself increasingly drawn to Nathan's easygoing nature, his quick wit, and the way he seemed genuinely interested in her thoughts.

At some point, Stacie and Mark excused themselves to hit the dance floor, but Penny and Nathan were so engrossed in their conversation that they barely noticed the two left the table. When Stacie and Mark returned to the table, looking tired but happy, they announced they were going home. "We stopped at the bar and settled the tab. You two stay and have fun," Stacie said, giving Penny a knowing smile."

Penny hugged her friends goodbye, her heart swelling with gratitude for their unwavering support. Not long after they left, the bar began to quiet down as the night stretched on, but they remained engrossed in their conversation—talking about everything from their favorite books to the best pizza in town. Time seemed to melt away.

When the manager approached their table with a gentle reminder that they were closing, Penny blinked in surprise. The once-crowded bar had emptied, leaving just the two of them in the cozy glow of the dim lights.

"Wow, we really lost track of time," Penny said, glancing around in disbelief.

Nathan smiled, leaning back in his chair. "I guess time flies when you're having fun."

Penny felt warmth bloom in her chest at his words, the night suddenly feeling more magical than she had anticipated. When she mentioned walking home, Nathan didn't hesitate.

"Mind if I walk with you?" he offered, standing up with an easy smile.

Penny's heart fluttered again as she nodded. "I'd like that."

They stepped out into the cool night air, the soft glow of the streetlights casting long shadows on the empty sidewalks. As they walked together, the quietness of the town felt intimate, their conversation weaving effortlessly between laughter and meaningful exchanges.

When they finally reached her house, Penny turned to Nathan, feeling both exhilarated and a little nervous. "Thanks for walking me home. Tonight was… it was really nice."

Nathan smiled, his gaze soft. "I had a great time too, Penny. Let's do this again soon?"

Penny felt her heart race as she handed him her phone to exchange numbers. As he entered his contact info, their fingers brushed, and the electricity of the moment made her pulse quicken.

With a smile, Nathan handed the phone back. "Goodnight, Penny."

"Goodnight, Nathan," she whispered, her heart still fluttering as she watched him walk down the street.

She stood there for a moment, savoring the night air and the memory of their evening together. Finally, she turned and headed inside, her heart light and her mind buzzing with the promise of what might come next.

She locked the door behind her and leaned against it, a dreamy smile on her face. Tonight, had been unexpected, but it was exactly what she needed. With a contented sigh, Penny headed to bed, already looking forward to the next time she would see Nathan.

KEL SUMMERS

CHAPTER FIVE

The next morning Penny blinked awake, feeling the comforting warmth of the sun's rays on her face. Stretching her arms overhead, there was an undeniable mix of excitement and determination, along with a bit of nervous energy buzzing inside her.

Today was all about preparation. As much as her thoughts kept drifting back to Nathan and their enchanting night together, she knew she had to keep her focus on her new job at the paper. The clock was ticking, and the reporter she was filling in for would be back from her leave in just a few short weeks. If she wanted to secure a permanent position, she needed to show Mr. Greely that she was indispensable.

With a sigh, Penny swung her legs out of bed and padded across the floor to the kitchen. She brewed a strong cup of coffee and settled at her desk, surrounded by stacks of notes and her laptop.

"Okay," she murmured to herself, glancing at the clock. "Time to make this count."

She started the day diving into how-to articles on reporting, headlines, and editing, immersing herself in the intricacies of newspaper journalism. She took notes, her fingers flying across the keyboard, absorbing tips that would set her apart as a valuable asset to the paper. Though a lot of it felt like a refresher from her community college courses, there was something comforting about solidifying her foundation.

After a few hours, Penny took a break, standing to stretch. Her muscles were tight from sitting, but her mind was flowing with inspiration. Moving on to the digital side of journalism, she researched strategies for print-to-digital transitions. Social media distribution, online storytelling, podcasting—the possibilities seemed endless. Stacie's comment about starting a podcast floated back into her mind. The idea of creating a podcast, especially with Stacie or Mark as her co-host, seemed like a fun and innovative project, and Penny found herself smiling at the thought of creating something fresh, something that could resonate with listeners. Plus, if it brought in some extra money through sponsors, all the better.

The day flew by in a blur of reading and note-taking. Penny was so engrossed in her research that she completely forgot about lunch. When she finally glanced at the clock, she realized it was almost dinnertime. Her eyes felt strained from hours of staring at the computer screen, and she decided it was time to put her work away for the night.

She headed to the kitchen, warming up a leftover meal, the comforting aroma filling the room. As she ate, Penny reviewed her to-do list for the day. Every box was checked off, and she felt a sense of accomplishment. She had laid a solid foundation for her future at the paper, and now it was time to relax.

Inspired by her evening with Nathan, Penny curled up on the couch and binged Smallville for the rest of the night. As she watched, her mind wandered back to Nathan. His warm smile, the way their conversation had flowed effortlessly. It was impossible not to think about him. Penny smiled to herself, the memory of their time together lingering.

"Maybe tomorrow," she whispered aloud, contemplating whether to text him. For now, she decided to text Mark and Stacie instead, inviting them over for a podcast brainstorming session. The thought of gathering with her friends to kick around ideas lifted her spirits even higher. Downsizing had been tough, but it had ignited a spark of motivation in her that she hadn't felt in a long time.

Just as Clark Kent was about to save the day yet again, her phone buzzed. Both Mark and Stacie had responded enthusiastically to her invite, and Penny felt a flutter of excitement. With her friends on board, she knew their brainstorming session would be productive and fun.

Determined to make the most of their meeting, Penny took to Pinterest, scrolling through endless ideas for snacks and decorations. She mentally inventoried her pantry, planning a menu that would impress her friends without requiring an early morning trip to the Farmer's Market.

She chuckled to herself, knowing that Mark and Stacie's excitement was likely driven 70% by curiosity about Nathan and 30% by the podcast. And that was just fine by her.

Later, after far too many comparisons between Nathan and the real Dean Cain, Penny decided her brain needed a break, and she headed off to bed. With a contented sigh, she sank into the pillows, pulling the blankets up under her chin, and her thoughts immediately drifted back to Nathan. His kind eyes and warm smile played over and over in her mind. Penny's heart fluttered as she remembered their conversation and how his laugh had made her feel at ease.

"Should I text him?" she wondered aloud, the question hanging in the still air.

Penny weighed the possibilities, her mind a whirlwind of excitement and doubt. She made a pact with herself, whispering softly, "If I don't hear from him this weekend, I'll text him on Monday after work."

Feeling a sense of resolve, Penny allowed herself to fully relax. The decision brought a wave of calm, and she felt the tension in her muscles melt away. She snuggled deeper into her blankets, the soft cotton soothing against her skin. The room's gentle darkness enveloped her, and her breathing slowed as she drifted closer to sleep.

The last conscious thought Penny had was of Nathan's smile. With that comforting image in her mind, she surrendered to a night of dreams filled with possibilities and the promise of what might come next.

Penny woke the next morning feeling refreshed and ready

to take on the day. After getting up and turning on her favorite Country Summer playlist, she brewed herself a strong cup of coffee and got to work preparing for her friends' arrival.

The kitchen became a lively hub of activity as Penny sliced fresh fruit, whipped up a batch of homemade guacamole, and arranged a cheese platter. The smells of fresh ingredients filled the space, creating an inviting atmosphere.

When Mark and Stacie arrived, their eyes were alive with curiosity and excitement. Stacie, unable to contain herself, burst through the door first, "Alright, spill it," she demanded. "Tell us everything!"

Penny laughed, ushering them in. "All in good time. Let's get some food first, then we'll talk."

They settled around the coffee table, diving into the spread Penny had prepared. The conversation flowed effortlessly, filled with laughter and excitement as they brainstormed potential names for the podcast, discussed different segments they could include, and explored ways to attract sponsors.

Mark's enthusiasm was contagious. "I'm telling you— this podcast is going to be huge! We could be the next big thing in the podcasting world."

Penny laughed, shaking her head. "Slow down, Mark. We're just in the beginning stages. Let's focus on getting the basics down first."

He grinned, unabashed. "Fine, fine. But just wait. We'll be award-winning podcasters in no time."

Stacie leaned forward, her eyes twinkling with amusement. "So, what's the theme? You mentioned something about scorn?"

Penny nodded, her excitement bubbling over. "Yes! Anything from women or men scorned by a lover to employees scorned by their employers. And we'll add a bit of pettiness in there, too. People aren't perfect. They get angry, and sometimes they want revenge. But honestly, isn't it usually the little, petty things that bug people the most?"

"Okay, I love this theme of pettiness," Mark said, tapping his fingers on the table. "Everyone wants to be petty sometimes, but sometimes I think they're too afraid to admit it."

Stacie nodded in agreement. "And we could have segments—maybe listeners could call in and share their stories of revenge or being scorned."

Penny smiled, feeling a surge of excitement as the ideas flowed. "Exactly! People aren't perfect, and sometimes they just need to vent. We can make it funny, and lighthearted, but also relatable."

By the time the snacks were gone, they had a solid outline for the podcast and they each had their assigned tasks for the upcoming week. Stacie leaned back, a contented smile on her face. "Okay, now that we've got that sorted—tell us about Nathan."

Penny blushed, her heart fluttering at the thought of him. She couldn't help the grin that spread across her face. "He's pretty amazing…"

Mark poured another round of drinks, leaning in with

curiosity. "Did he tell you how long he's sticking around town?"

"He said it's still up in the air. He's not sure how much longer this project for his family is going to take," Penny explained, feeling a warmth spread through her as she talked about him. "I do hope he stays a while. It's been fun getting to know him."

Stacie raised an eyebrow. "Has he texted?"

Penny shook her head, a hint of uncertainty creeping in. "Not yet. I thought about texting him, but I decided to wait until after work tomorrow. If I haven't heard from him by then, I'll text him."

"Oh my gosh! Work! I nearly forgot about that. Are you excited?" Stacie was clearly excited for her friend. "I almost want to send Mr. Novak a thank-you card from you. If it weren't for him, maybe none of this would be happening."

"Tomorrow is going to be one of the best days of your life," Mark said confidently, raising his glass in a toast. "To new beginnings and endless possibilities."

"To new beginnings," Penny echoed, clinking her glass with theirs.

Later, after they'd said their goodbyes and Penny was left alone in the quiet of her house, she found herself more excited than ever. Tomorrow would be the start of something new. She barely slept that night, her mind buzzing with anticipation about the podcast, her new job, and the potential of something special with Nathan.

Penny barely slept, her mind racing with anticipation and

excitement for her first day at the newspaper. Long before the sun even considered rising, she was already wide awake, the early morning silence of her bedroom filled only with the sound of her rapid heartbeat. She knew the code to the back door of the newspaper office and toyed with the idea of arriving super early. The thought of stepping into her new role made her feel like a child on Christmas morning, but she didn't want to seem overanxious.

After a few futile attempts at getting back to sleep, she gave up and decided to make the most of her extra time. She tried calling her parents to share the good news, but the call went straight to voicemail. Leaving a cheerful message, she ended with, "I can't wait to tell you all about it when we catch up!"

With plenty of time on her hands, Penny found herself doing things she usually never bothered with. She made her bed with meticulous care, smoothing out every wrinkle in the comforter. "Who even vacuums before work?" she muttered as she ran the vacuum across her living room carpet, surprised to find the hum of the machine oddly soothing.

Satisfied with her efforts and knowing that she would come home to a neat and tidy house later, Penny turned her attention to her outfit. She slipped into the navy-blue pixie pants and cream-colored peasant top that she had laid out the night before. The silky soft fabric felt comforting against her skin and was a tangible reminder of her new beginning. She opted for ballerina flats instead of heels because there was no telling where the story would take her today. She was giddy as she imagined herself following down a lead to a juicy story.

Standing in front of the mirror, Penny took a deep breath and let out a little squeal of excitement. The reflection looking back at her was of someone ready to tackle whatever the day had in store. "This is it," she whispered to herself, feeling another round of excitement surge through her.

Checking the clock on the stove, she saw that it was finally a reasonable time to leave without seeming too crazy and overeager. She grabbed her laptop bag, slung it over her shoulder, and headed out the door, locking it behind her. The early morning air was crisp and invigorating, and the sky was just beginning to brighten with the promise of a new day.

The drive to the newspaper office felt surreal. Penny navigated through the quiet streets, the familiar landmarks passing by in a blur. Her thoughts were a whirlwind of possibilities and what-ifs, each one more exciting than the last. She arrived at the parking lot, her heart fluttering with a mix of nerves and exhilaration.

Stepping out of her car, Penny took a moment to steady herself. The parking lot was already full, which struck her as odd for such an early hour. She furrowed her brow, wondering if she had missed some important memo. She laughed and reminded herself that she wouldn't have received a memo yet. Then she laughed more, thinking they were probably there for her first official day. She was joking, of course, but that would be pretty cool. Whatever it was, nothing could ruin her day.

Grabbing a box of personal items and her laptop bag, Penny considered bringing along the familiar decorations from her cubicle at Novak's. But she decided against it. At Novak's, she had more room due to the partition walls, whereas here, she would only have a desk. Besides, she felt superstitious about bringing anything with potential bad juju from her old job, so she'd left it all behind.

As she approached the back door, her phone rang. She glanced at the screen and saw it was her dad. She opted to call him back once she had settled in, assuming he was just returning her call from earlier. She made her way to the back door, punched in the code, and walked inside, the familiar scent of newsprint and coffee greeting her like an old friend.

She turned the corner, unable to wipe the grin off her face. But as she stepped inside, her smile faltered. The atmosphere was thick with tension, and the usually bustling newsroom was eerily quiet. Penny's eyes scanned the room, and her breath caught in her throat. There was a reason everyone was there early, and from the tears and red-rimmed eyes, it didn't look like a happy reason.

Something was very, very wrong.

CHAPTER SIX

"Oh, honey. Did you hear the news?" Daphne came rushing over to Penny, her usual sunny demeanor replaced by tear-streaked cheeks and her trembling hands clutching a tissue.

Penny stood there with a big dumb grin on her face while everyone else looked like someone had died. "No, Daphne. What happened?" she asked as she looked around for Mr. Greely. When she didn't see him, she felt her stomach drop. Instantly she knew something big had happened, and she was crossing all her fingers and toes that it hadn't happened to him.

"Daphne, what's going on?" Penny's voice quivered as she took in the tear-streaked faces around her.

Her eyes puffy from crying, Daphne reached out and gently guided Penny to an empty desk. Bonnie appeared at her side. Her presence was both comforting and ominous. After Penny had set her things down, Bonnie wrapped her in a hug, and Penny knew the news was as bad as she feared.

Bonnie pulled back, and Penny saw that her eyes were filled with sorrow. "Penny, Mr. Greely had a heart attack yesterday. He didn't make it."

The words hit her like a punch to the gut, leaving her breathless. Penny felt the world tilt beneath her feet, and she gripped the desk for support. Her vision blurred, and for a second, she felt as though she might collapse.

Her phone rang, the sound slicing through the heavy atmosphere like a knife. Penny glanced down at the screen, her dad's name flashing. She fumbled to answer, already knowing why he was calling.

"Dad?" Her voice wavered, barely above a whisper.

"I tried calling earlier, sweetheart. Are you at the paper? Have you heard about Mr. Greely?" Her father's voice, thick with emotion, mirrored her own grief.

"I just heard, Dad," Penny said, her voice breaking. "I'm so sorry. I know you were close."

A long, shaky breath came from the other end of the line. "We played golf just last week… I can't believe it. He seemed so healthy."

"I know," Penny whispered, her throat tight. "Dad, I just got to the paper. I'll call you back once I know more, okay?"

"Yes, sure. I'm sorry. I thought you would be at work by now. I didn't know you were going into the paper today."

Penny sighed, the weight of everything pressing down on her. "It's a bit of a long story. I'll tell you all about it when I call later."

"Okay. Love you, honey."

"Love you too." She ended the call, her hand trembling as she slid the phone back into her pocket. The tears she had been holding back finally spilled over, hot and unstoppable. She felt like she was drowning in a sea of disbelief and sorrow, struggling to come to terms with the fact that Mr. Greely—kind, steady Mr. Greely—was gone.

Bonnie touched her arm gently. "It's hard to believe, isn't it?"

Penny nodded numbly, trying to hold herself together. Memories of her last conversation with him flashed through her mind—the warmth in his voice, the pride he'd shown in her work. She had been so excited to work with him, to prove herself, and now...

She wiped at her tears, her heart aching as she thought of Mr. Greely's quiet office, the way he always had a cup of black coffee by his side as he reviewed the latest drafts. And now the paper—his life's work—was left without its captain.

Penny glanced at Daphne, seeing fresh tears streaming down her face. Rumors had swirled about Daphne and Mr. Greely having a thing on the side, but now wasn't the time for such thoughts. Her mind, however, was racing in a million different directions, struggling to process the shock.

"What's going to happen to the paper?" Penny's voice trembled with a mixture of fear and disbelief.

Daphne dabbed at her eyes with the crumpled tissue,

shaking her head. "We don't know yet. Everyone's been asking the same thing."

Penny tried to imagine the future of the paper. Surely, someone would be put in as acting editor until a formal plan was made. But who? The paper was owned and operated by the Greely family, and as far as she knew, no other members of the Greely family lived nearby. Then she remembered Mr. Greely's nephew. Maybe he would take over. She supposed Mr. Greely had arrangements for his death, but what did she know about such things? She didn't even have a savings account, let alone a will.

Bonnie joined them, her eyes red and swollen. She blew her nose loudly, trying to compose herself. "I heard his nephew is going to be the acting editor. Remember? I told you about him. It sounds like he wants to convert everything to digital by the end of the year. Which is what I was afraid of. I can make the switch, but it will upset our subscribers."

Penny's heart sank further. "You're kidding me? That's not what Mr. Greely wanted either. I can see adding digital, but getting rid of the printed paper altogether—does that make sense? Especially when we have such a large subscription base."

Bonnie shook her head, the reality of the situation settling over them like a dark cloud. "It's not what he wanted at all. He believed in the printed word. He thought there was something special about holding a newspaper, feeling the pages in your hands."

Penny nodded, a lump forming in her throat. "I agree. There's a connection with the readers, something tangible. Going fully digital would eliminate that."

Daphne looked between them, and her eyes filled with uncertainty. "Do you think his nephew will listen to us? I mean, we know what our readers want."

Penny sighed, her mind churning with worry and determination. "I don't know, but we have to try. I mean, I know his nephew is family. But we know what Mr. Greely wanted, and we have to fight for his vision and what he built."

Just then, Daphne's eyes widened, and she glanced past Penny with a look of urgency. "Excuse me for a moment," Daphne murmured, quickly stepping away.

Before Penny could turn to see what had caught Daphne's attention, a tall man wearing a hideous plaid jacket, and a warm smile approached them and introduced himself to Penny.

"Hi, you must be Penny. I'm Carl, the sports editor. I've heard your name mentioned quite a bit."

Penny shook his hand, feeling a bit of relief at the distraction. "Nice to meet you, Carl. It's been... a rough morning."

Carl nodded, his expression sympathetic. "I can imagine. Mr. Greely was a big fan of yours. He always spoke highly of your writing."

Penny felt a mix of pride and sadness. "Thank you. That means a lot coming from him."

Carl gestured to the empty chairs nearby. "Would you mind if I joined you? We're all trying to process this together."

Bonnie nodded, her eyes still glistening with unshed tears. "Please do. We were just talking about what might happen next."

As Carl settled into the chair, Penny glanced over her shoulder, curious about who had drawn Daphne away so urgently. Her attention snapped back to their little group when she heard Bonnie let out a sudden gasp.

"What happened at your meeting? Did Mr. Greely hire you? I'm guessing he did since you're here this morning and have a box with you."

Penny opened her mouth to respond, then remembered she hadn't signed any paperwork. Depending on who took over, would they even know that she had been hired on Thursday? Even if they didn't, surely the others could vouch for her. She thought back to her shopping spree, heart pounding with worry. She had already cut all the tags off her new clothes. Panicking, she scanned the room for Daphne. Should she say something now or wait? Everyone was clearly in distress. Maybe it was better to play along now and talk with the acting editor when they arrived.

"He did," Penny said, forcing a smile. "I'm supposed to start today, filling in for Mallory while she's on leave."

"Oh, perfect," Bonnie replied with a touch of relief. "Wait until you meet her. She's sweet. I think you know everyone else now that you've met Carl. Well, except for Mr. Greely's nephew. I'm assuming he will be here shortly."

Not quite trusting her voice, Penny just nodded. Mr. Greely had a habit of writing everything down in the planner on his desk. She was sure he would have written down her hire date or mentioned it to Daphne. Or was that just wishful thinking? The uncertainty gnawed at her. She looked around again, and spotted Daphne following someone out of the newsroom, but she hadn't turned in time to see who it was.

Penny tried to tune into Bonnie and Carl's conversation, but her mind kept drifting back to Mr. Greely, wondering if he'd told anyone he'd hired her. She felt a sinking dread in her stomach, unsure what would happen to her. Her phone buzzed in her pocket, breaking her thoughts. It was a group text from Mark and Stacie. The news had spread quickly through their small town, and they were checking on her.

Hey. We heard the news about Mr. Greely. We're very sorry. How are you holding up?

Penny texted back with trembling fingers.

I'm freaking out a little. I think I'm still in shock. I can't believe he's gone. I'm not sure if he told anyone about the job.

She reached for her blue tiger's eye necklace, holding the stone tightly in her hand. It was one of her gran's favorites. The stone was for protection, power, and perseverance—all things she desperately needed right now. She focused on her breathing —slow and deep—trying to calm the storm of anxiety swirling inside her.

Bonnie elbowed her gently and nodded toward the front of the newsroom. Penny heard Carl mumble, "There he is. Mr. Greely's nephew. She looked to where Bonnie was pointing and nearly passed out. *No. No, no, no. This couldn't be. This wasn't happening.* She scanned the room, half-expecting her friends to jump out and yell, "Gotcha!" But the solemn faces around her confirmed the truth. The room went silent as Daphne stepped forward and spoke in a soft but steady voice.

"Everyone, this is Nathan Greely, Mr. Greely's nephew. He will be acting editor-in-chief until the estate is settled. For now, he's in charge."

Bonnie leaned in and whispered, "I told you he was cute. I just hope he listens to us about the digital transition."

Penny's mind was reeling, and she was barely able to manage a quick nod. She wished for an invisibility cloak or to be hit by a shrink ray. Anything to escape the moment. Maybe if she stood still enough, he wouldn't notice her. But Daphne had other plans.

"If you would, please state your name for Mr. Greely and tell him what you do here. He's met most of you since he's been in and out the past few months, but he might not remember your names. Penny, let's start with you."

Bonnie gently pushed her forward, and Penny felt the heat rising in her face. Their eyes met, and she saw the recognition spark in his.

Clearing her throat, she managed to speak, though it felt like her insides were twisting. "I'm Penny. I'm a reporter. It's nice to meet you."

Her mind racing, she tried to shrink back into the crowd as quickly as possible. This was either a good thing or a complete disaster.

Nathan looked momentarily confused but quickly recovered, flashing his Superman smile. "It's nice to meet you too, Penny."

The room buzzed with quiet conversations as everyone introduced themselves to Nathan, but Penny's mind was in chaos. She couldn't believe this twist of fate. She had no idea what it meant for her future at the paper, but she knew one thing for sure—her life had just gotten a lot more complicated.

KEL SUMMERS

CHAPTER SEVEN

Penny had never felt more mortified in her life. Sweat beaded on her upper lip, and her heart raced as if it might burst from her chest. Her breaths came shallow and quick, and she was fairly certain she was one step away from a full-blown panic attack. *Why was she so upset? Nothing happened. All they did was talk*, she thought to herself. *But still...*

She scanned the room, her eyes darting from face to face, catching glimpses of curious looks and raised eyebrows. She could feel the weight of their unspoken questions pressing down on her. Her vision blurred as her panic intensified. Desperate for an escape, she mumbled an incoherent "excuse me," and hurried from the newsroom, her footsteps echoing in her wake.

The bathroom door swung open with a thud, the sound reverberating in the silence. Stumbling to the sink, she gripped the edge, her knuckles white, and stared at her reflection in the mirror.

"Get it together, Penny," she whispered to woman staring back at her. Her cheeks were flushed, her eyes wide and filled with panic. She splashed cold water on her face, the chill shocking her system and momentarily soothing the heat that had risen to her skin. The cool water dripped from her chin as she leaned forward, trying to calm the storm inside her.

With trembling hands, she pulled out her phone and quickly typed a message to Mark and Stacie.

> *I'm freaking out. Just saw Nathan. He's Mr. Greely's nephew!!*

She hit send, and clung to the hope that their responses would bring her some semblance of calm. Leaning back against the bathroom wall, Penny closed her eyes and tried to imagine them there beside her—Stacie's knowing smile and Mark's ever-present sarcasm. The image gave her a sliver of comfort.

When she opened her eyes again, she looked at herself in the mirror, her normally bright, confident eyes now shadowed with fear. "This can't be real," she muttered, shaking her head as if the motion would wake her from this nightmare. But the sharp pain in her hip, where she'd accidentally slammed into the counter, confirmed she wasn't dreaming. This was her reality.

Penny forced herself to take slow, deep breaths, trying to steer clear of her normal fatalistic thinking. She replayed their conversations from Friday in her mind. Did he mention anything about the newspaper? Did she? It seemed like they had talked about everything. How did this not come up?

"Calm down, Penny," she told her reflection sternly, her voice barely above a whisper. "We're both adults. You can handle this situation without drama." She gave herself a determined nod, straightened her blouse, and pushed through the metal door, letting it swing shut behind her with a heavy clang.

The newsroom bustled with activity, a stark contrast to the chaos in her mind. She grabbed a bottle of water from the fridge, the cold seeping into her palms, grounding her as she twisted off the cap and took a long sip. The meeting had ended while she was having her mini-breakdown, and everyone had dispersed and were now engrossed in their tasks for the day.

But Penny still felt like an outsider, unsure if she truly belonged there. Her eyes scanned the room, landing on Daphne at her desk, the older woman's worried gaze meeting hers. Thankfully, Nathan was nowhere to be seen. For now, at least, she could breathe a little easier.

The newsroom was alive with the hum of printers and the clatter of keyboards. It was a familiar soundtrack in Penny's life, but today it felt more like a cacophony of disarray echoing the turmoil in her mind. She made her way across the room, trying to blend in and avoid drawing attention to herself. Yet, as she approached Daphne's desk, she couldn't escape the concern etched on the face of the woman she had known almost her entire life.

"Penny, are you okay?" Daphne asked. Her voice was soft and full of worry. She looked up from her computer, her eyes scanning Penny's face with genuine concern. "You look pale. I know this is a hard day for all of us. I just... well, it's just so awful. I already miss him so much.

Penny's heart sank as the reality came crashing down on

her. *Mr. Greely has passed away.* How had she managed to let herself forget, even for a moment? Mr. Greely, her friend and mentor, was gone. She had been so consumed with anxiety over his nephew Nathan's presence, but now the true loss hit her like a tidal wave.

She cast her gaze toward Mr. Greely's office, where the door was closed, and the desk sat empty. A poignant emptiness seemed to fill the space where his boisterous laugh and warm advice had once resided. The weight of guilt pressed down on her shoulders. How could she have been so wrapped up in her own world when the man who had been like a second father to her was no longer there? She silently hoped he had known how much she appreciated him.

"I'm okay, Daphne," Penny replied, her voice thick with emotion. "It's just going to be strange not seeing him here. He made a tremendous difference in my life. This place won't ever be the same without him."

Daphne reached out, her warm hand patting Penny's, offering a comfort that words couldn't quite capture. "He adored you, Penny. He loved you like you were his own," she said, her voice filled with sincerity.

The words touched Penny deeply, sparking a bittersweet sense of gratitude and loss. She swallowed hard, blinking back tears, then suddenly remembered the reason she had approached Daphne in the first place. Her career felt as precarious as a house of cards in a gale.

"Daphne, when I was in here last week, did Mr. Greely

mention his plans for me?" Penny asked, anxiety creeping back into her voice.

Daphne looked at her with confusion, and Penny's heart sank further. *This wasn't good. No, not good at all.*

"He wanted me to come in full-time, to cover for Mallory while she's on leave. Please tell me he started the paperwork, or at least told you about it," Penny pleaded, desperation seeping into her words.

Daphne's brow furrowed in confusion, and Penny's stomach twisted into knots. "He didn't say anything to me about it," Daphne said slowly. "But don't worry. Just talk to Nathan. I'm sure he'll understand. Mr. Greely trusted you."

The thought of confronting Nathan about her job made her heart race again, panic rising in her throat. The idea of having to plead her case to him after what had happened between them was enough to make her want to crawl back into the bathroom and hide.

"Do you want me to let him know you need to speak with him?" Daphne offered gently.

Penny nodded, though the thought of facing him made her stomach churn. "Yeah, that'd be good," she managed to say, her voice barely steady.

Daphne gave her a sympathetic smile. "He's meeting with the printing team right now, but I'll make sure he knows you need to talk when he's done."

With a weak smile in return, Penny wandered away, feeling

the weight of uncertainty pressing down on her shoulders. She scanned the room for a place to settle, her nerves still jangling. Out of the corner of her eye, she saw Bonnie waving her over.

"Come on, sit with me," Bonnie called, gesturing to the desk across from her. "Mallory won't mind if you use her desk while she's out. It'll be good to have some company."

Grateful for the refuge, Penny sat down and sank into the chair. The newsroom buzzed around her, but for the first time that day, she felt a small sense of stability. She had a desk, a space, and someone who wanted her there.

Penny sat at Mallory's desk, the constant clatter of keyboards and ringing phones creating a rhythm that was somehow both comforting and unsettling. She shifted her gaze from her laptop to the room around her, trying to ground herself in the familiarity of the newsroom's organized chaos. The hum of conversations and the rustle of paper filled the air, but Penny's thoughts were elsewhere.

Across from her, Bonnie sat at her desk, her eyes flicking up from her screen to catch Penny's gaze. "Hey," she said gently. "Are you okay? You took off so quickly after meeting Nathan. I thought you might be sick."

Penny let out a low moan and slumped back in her chair, covering her face with her hands. "Define okay," she muttered, her voice muffled by her hands.

Bonnie swiveled her chair around, giving Penny her full attention. Her eyes were wide, and her brow furrowed with concern. "Alright, what's going on? I mean, aside from the obvious. You and Mr. Greely have known each other forever. This must be hitting you pretty hard. If you need to take a breather or start fresh another day, I'm sure no one would mind."

Penny groaned louder, peeking out from behind her fingers to meet Bonnie's gaze. "That's the problem. Mr. Greely didn't mention anything to Daphne about hiring me full-time. I might not even have a job here."

Bonnie's eyes widened, her mouth falling open in shock. "Oh no, Penny. But we need you and you've been here forever. Surely Mr. Greely's nephew will see that."

Penny managed a weak smile at Bonnie's attempt at optimism. But of course, Bonnie didn't know the other piece of the puzzle—about her and Nathan. That whole mess complicated things further, adding another layer to her anxiety.

"My opinion?" Bonnie continued, leaning in closer, as if sharing a secret. "Act like you work here until someone tells you that you don't. Do you know where the article board is?"

Penny shook her head, feeling a little lost. "I've seen it, but I don't know how to read it. It looks like it's all in code."

Bonnie grinned and stood up, beckoning for Penny to follow her. They made their way across the room, weaving between desks and bustling coworkers until they reached the far wall, where a large board displayed a colorful array of sticky notes and index cards.

"This is it," Bonnie said, gesturing with a flourish. "Each reporter is color-coded, see? The subject lines show the due dates and other important stuff. Here, let me show you."

Bonnie took an orange marker from a nearby holder and added Penny's initials to a few notes marked with Mallory's color. Penny watched, and a sense of gratitude swelled in her chest. It felt good to have someone in her corner, especially when everything else felt so uncertain.

"See?" Bonnie said, stepping back with a satisfied nod. "If we believe it's true, so will everyone else."

Penny nodded, feeling a flicker of hope. Bonnie's support meant more than she could express. They'd known each other in school, sure, but had never run in the same circles. Yet now, Penny needed allies more than ever, and Bonnie seemed willing to be just that.

"Thank you, Bonnie," Penny said, her voice earnest. "I really appreciate this."

"Anytime," Bonnie replied with a smile. "Now, let's get you settled."

Penny smiled faintly, but the lingering dread remained. She needed to talk to Nathan, to figure out where she stood. But for now, sitting at Mallory's desk, surrounded by the hum of the newsroom, she let herself believe she belonged. Even if just for a little while.

The steady rhythm of work became her refuge. She lost herself in drafting potential stories, sifting through leads, and reviewing notes from past assignments. Hours blurred together, and for a moment, she forgot about everything, Nathan, Mr.

Greely's loss, her uncertain future. The newsroom's clatter became a welcome background to her thoughts, a comforting hum in an otherwise chaotic day.

But then the phone rang, pulling her out of her concentration. Penny picked up the receiver, her heart skipping a beat as Daphne's voice came through.

"Penny, Mr. Greely can see you now."

KEL SUMMERS

CHAPTER EIGHT

Penny exhaled slowly, trying to ease the knot of tension that had been building in her shoulders. She knew there was no avoiding the inevitable, no running away from the conversation that had to happen. With another steadying breath, she stood, her legs feeling unsteady as though they might betray her at any moment, and made her way toward Nathan's office.

Her mind raced, attempting to organize her thoughts into a coherent argument. *How do I prove myself? How do I make him see that I'm worth the risk?* She had spent the entire weekend studying digital media, trying to prepare herself for this very moment that she didn't know was coming, and now it all boiled down to the next few minutes.

Standing outside Nathan's office, Penny hesitated. The wooden door, which once felt like a welcome threshold between mentor and mentee when Mr. Greely sat behind it, now loomed as an ominous barrier. She vividly remembered sitting in this room with him, laughing over egg salad sandwiches, her future seemingly bright. Now, everything was uncertain.

Summoning her courage, she raised her hand and knocked. The sound reverberated through the silence like a drumbeat signaling a pivotal moment.

"Come in," Nathan's voice called from within. It was calm, firm—almost too controlled, Penny thought.

She pushed the door open, stepping into the office that felt both familiar and strange without Mr. Greely's presence. The door clicked softly shut behind her, and in that instant, Penny wished for anything—a fire alarm, a power outage, something to delay the conversation that lay ahead. But there was no such intervention. She had to face whatever came next.

Nathan sat behind the desk. His posture was relaxed yet authoritative. The room seemed smaller with him there, as though the very air had shifted to accommodate his presence. He glanced up from a stack of papers, his expression unreadable, though his eyes flickered with something Penny couldn't quite place—curiosity, perhaps, or maybe calculation.

"Have a seat," he gestured to the chairs opposite him.

Penny's pulse quickened as she complied, settling into one of the chairs. The air between them was thick with awkward tension, a tension that carried the weight of their history—just days ago, they had been laughing together, and now the memory of that night hung between them like an unspoken secret. She could still feel the warmth of his hand on the small of her back as he walked her home, the unexpected connection, and it made sitting across from him now all the more disorienting.

Nathan leaned back in his chair, folding his hands together

as he studied her. "I think it's safe to say," he began slowly, his voice measured, "this is a bit of an awkward situation."

Penny managed a tight smile. *Understatement of the century*, she thought.

"I was planning to call yesterday," he continued, his tone softening, "but given the circumstances, I'm sure you understand why I didn't."

Penny swallowed, her mouth suddenly dry. "I understand," she said, her voice quieter than she intended. "I'm so sorry for your loss. Your uncle… he meant a lot to me. He was an incredible mentor."

Nathan's expression softened slightly, though his eyes remained guarded. "Thank you. I appreciate that."

He rocked forward in his chair, the movement abrupt and almost startling. Penny's heart skipped a beat, and she forced herself to breathe, to remain composed despite the tension knotting in her stomach.

Calm down, girl, she silently reminded herself, inhaling deeply through her nose and exhaling slowly through her mouth.

The office was quiet. The only sound was the soft hum of the air conditioning and the occasional creak of Nathan's chair. Penny shifted slightly in her seat, the fabric rustling beneath her as she tried to project an air of confidence she didn't quite feel.

She could sense the weight of Nathan's gaze on her, searching and assessing. It was clear that he was considering not just her qualifications, but perhaps the deeper implications of their current predicament. Penny squared her shoulders, meeting his eyes with as much resolve as she could muster.

It was an awkward few seconds before he spoke again. "I'm not certain what to do about this situation," he began, his voice carrying the weight of someone who had rehearsed this speech in his mind but still found it difficult to say aloud. "Daphne tells me you were here last week, and my uncle offered you a full-time position. Is that correct?"

Penny's thoughts raced as she remembered Bonnie's advice: act as though you belong. Steeling herself, she nodded, her voice steady despite the butterflies swirling in her stomach. "Yes, he wanted me to start today. He planned for me to fill in for Mallory while she's on leave. I spent the weekend preparing and working on her upcoming tasks. I have a pretty good start on them."

Nathan nodded, his gaze drifting down to the stack of papers on his desk. He rifled through them, a frown furrowing his brow. "The issue is… there's no formal record of that offer." His tone was neutral, but Penny could sense the finality behind his words. "I've reviewed the numbers, and with the shift I'm planning for the paper, I don't see how we can justify adding to the print division right now."

Penny's stomach lurched as if the ground beneath her had suddenly disappeared. *No. This can't be happening.* She fought to keep the rising panic from her voice. "I know you're leaning toward going strictly digital," she said, her voice carrying a quiet desperation. "And after doing some research, I can certainly see the benefits of that decision. But no matter what direction you choose, I'm a talented writer. I've been with the paper for a long time. My column is very popular."

Nathan regarded her for a moment, his expression unreadable. "Your column has been well-received, but..." He paused, choosing his words carefully. "As of now, it's been done on a freelance basis. You're not officially part of the team. And while I appreciate your enthusiasm for digital, I have to be honest—I don't see how your current role fits into my vision for the future of the paper."

Penny's heart sank, her pulse thudding in her ears. "So... what are you saying?" she asked, though she already feared the answer.

"I'm saying that, for now, we'll have to put your column on hold. If things change, we'll reach out. But I can't make any promises." His voice was firm, businesslike, as though the decision had already been made.

Penny felt as though she had been punched in the gut. She felt a lump rise in her throat as she tried to process what he was saying. "But... I was counting on this job. I've always been loyal to the paper. I love working here."

Nathan's expression remained impassive, his eyes distant and cool, a stark contrast to the warmth she had seen in him before. "But you don't actually work here, now do you?"

His question, filled with condescension cut through her like a knife. Penny clenched her fists, her nails digging into her palms as she fought to keep her emotions in check. She knew this wasn't the place to let her temper get the best of her.

"I'm sorry this didn't work out." She heard him say. "I hope you understand it's not personal."

But it *was* personal. How could it not be? Penny swallowed back the sting of tears, refusing to let them fall in front of him. She stood, her hands trembling at her sides. "Thank you for your time," she said, her voice stiff, formal. "Please let me know if anything changes."

Without waiting for his response, she turned and walked out of the office, her vision blurred by the tears she could no longer hold back. The newsroom felt like a blur as she moved through it, barely registering the concerned glances from her would-be coworkers. She felt numb, as though the weight of the rejection had hollowed her out from the inside.

Back at her desk, Penny hastily gathered her belongings, her hands shaking as she shoved notebooks and papers into her bag. She was grateful that Bonnie wasn't at her desk—she wasn't ready to face anyone just yet.

The moment she stepped outside, the cool air hit her like a splash of water, and the floodgates opened. Hot tears streamed down her face, and she wiped at them furiously, ashamed of her vulnerability.

She didn't look back as she headed to her Jeep, her mind swirling with the realization that she had just lost her second job in less than two weeks.

CHAPTER NINE

Once inside the privacy of her Jeep, Penny let the dam break. She pounded the steering wheel with her fists, her sobs coming in great, heaving gasps. Hot tears streamed down her face, blurring the world outside her windshield into a wash of color and light as she pulled out of the parking lot and headed home. The day had gone so horribly wrong, and her mind couldn't grasp how quickly her future had been ripped out from under her.

What am I going to do now? she thought, her breath hitching in her throat.

She had been so sure. When Mr. Greely offered her the position, everything had seemed to fall into place—her dreams of working full-time at the paper, the sense of purpose she'd been missing, the security that came with a paycheck. She had spent a small fortune last Thursday, certain that her future at the paper was secure. But now? That cushion of three months' severance from Novak felt like it was slipping away faster than she could catch it.

Penny pulled into her driveway, the sight of her familiar,

quiet house doing little to calm her racing heart. She sat there for a moment, her hands gripping the steering wheel tightly, her breathing still ragged from crying. *Get inside,* she told herself. *You need to calm down.*

The minute she opened her front door, the gentle scent of lavender from her diffuser hit her, a small comfort in the storm of emotions swirling inside her. She closed the door softly behind her, leaning against it for support, and let out a deep breath.

Her phone buzzed in her bag, interrupting the stillness. Penny fumbled for it, wiping her tear-streaked face with the back of her hand as she glanced at the screen. It was Stacie.

How's the first day going with Superman?

Penny groaned softly, unable to face Stacie's well-meaning text. She left the message unread, her thumb hovering over the reply button before she set the phone down on the kitchen counter. *Not now, Stacie.* She knew that if she told her friend what had happened, Stacie would drop everything and rush over. Penny loved her for that, but she wasn't ready to face anyone—not yet.

Her stomach churned with nausea, whether from stress or the lack of lunch, she couldn't tell. She made her way to the fridge, hoping to find something, anything, to ease the gnawing emptiness inside her. Her eyes settled on a package of tortellini—a comfort food she often turned to when everything else felt like it was falling apart.

The familiar routine of boiling water, mixing the creamy

marinara and alfredo sauces, and tearing off a piece of baguette provided a much-needed distraction. Penny stirred the sauce into the tortellini, the act of cooking soothing her frazzled nerves ever so slightly.

She peeled off her work clothes, replacing them with her soft leggings and an oversized sweatshirt, the kind of outfit that let her hide from the world, where she could be herself without pretending to be okay. She stared at the steam rising from the pot on the stove, watching it swirl against the kitchen window like the haze of confusion that clouded her mind.

Once the food was ready, she settled onto the couch, pulling a throw blanket over her legs, and ate in silence. The warm, creamy tortellini was a temporary comfort, but it wasn't enough to quiet the storm raging inside her. The tears threatened to spill again as she set her half-empty bowl aside. In a surge of frustration, Penny grabbed her phone, deleted Nathan's number, and tossed it onto the coffee table with a heavy thud. *Good riddance.*

Her laptop sat open on the arm of the couch, and Penny stared at it for a moment before logging in. The job search began again, a sea of listings that all seemed the same. As she scrolled through page after page, her mind wandered, calculating how long she could survive on her severance. ***A month, maybe two, if I'm careful.*** Her parents would help her if it came to that, but the thought of asking them felt like admitting defeat. She wasn't ready for that—not yet.

Her phone dinged. Stacie again.

Hey, how are you?

Penny's fingers hovered over the keyboard. *What do I even say?* She took a deep breath and typed, "Today has not been the best day. Actually, the past week has been one giant roller coaster. I'm wondering what I need to do to get off this ride."

The response was almost immediate. "Oh, honey. What's wrong? Bad first day? I'm sure it was weird not having Mr. Greely there. I can't believe he's gone."

Penny felt the tears welling up again, her throat tightening. She could barely type out her reply. "It was the first day that never happened. Mr. Greely didn't tell anyone he hired me. No paperwork means no job."

The dots blinked on the screen for what felt like an eternity before Stacie's message came through. "No! No way. I'm so sorry, Penny. What can I do?"

Penny smiled faintly, her heart warmed by Stacie's fierce loyalty. "I don't think there's much anyone can do right now. I've spent the afternoon trying to figure out what comes next, but so far, I've got nothing."

Without missing a beat, Stacie responded, "Superman's got some nerve. If I knew where he lived, I'd TP his house."

Penny laughed through her tears. Stacie's anger warmed Penny's heart. It was a sign of a true friend. It also made Penny feel better about her own anger.

"I don't want to hear no for an answer. Mark and I will be there after work. We can help you brainstorm." Stacie's firm and unyielding insistence came through the phone.

She was right. Penny's first instinct was to say no. She had always had a hard time letting others see her upset or asking for help… even when she knew she needed it.

"Thank you," she finally replied. "I probably need some help. Right now, I'm just trying not to lose my mind."

Hanging up, Penny set her phone down and surveyed her house. It was cluttered with the remnants of her earlier despair: discarded clothes, empty dishes, and the laptop still open to job listings. It didn't quite look like a tornado had hit, but almost.

She stood and began tidying up, rinsing the dishes, and stacking them neatly in the sink. In the bathroom, she splashed water on her face, the coolness reviving her spirits slightly. She examined her reflection, noting the puffiness of her eyes and the blotchy redness of her cheeks.

With a deep breath, Penny forced a smile, reminding herself that this was not the worst thing that could happen to her—not by a long shot. The universe had to have another plan for her—a better plan, and she needed to be ready for it when it came through.

She straightened her shoulders and resolved to face whatever came next with renewed determination.

KEL SUMMERS

CHAPTER TEN

Penny's living room was filled with the rich scent of takeout—spicy wings, cheesy pizza, and something sweet she couldn't quite place yet—and the warm presence of her best friends,

As soon as they had stepped through the door, Penny wrapped them both in a tight, lingering hug, her chest rising and falling with a deep, exhausted sigh. That hug, filled with the weight of unspoken emotions, felt like the only thing holding her together.

Stacie's eyes shimmered, a tear or two threatening to escape, as she held Penny close for an extra beat. "No more tears, okay?" Penny said with a soft, shaky laugh, pulling back and swiping at her damp eyes. "I've cried enough for all of us to last a lifetime. I'm choosing to believe there's something better right around the corner."

Stacie gave a firm nod, though her lips trembled as she blinked away her own tears. Mark, standing a little off to the side, offered a characteristic smirk. "Oh, no. I'm allergic to this much emotion," he teased, his eyes betraying his concern. Holding up a bag of chips and a bottle of pre-mixed margaritas like trophies, he added, "Let's drown whatever's left of your sorrows in carbs and questionable life choices."

Penny couldn't help but chuckle. This was exactly what she needed—a night of food, laughter, and friends. She ushered them into the cozy living room, where the couch and a worn rocking chair awaited, just like always. Stacie dropped onto the couch next to Penny, sinking into the cushions, while Mark made a beeline for the old rocking chair, which groaned under his weight.

Once they were all situated, Stacie leaned forward, her hands clasped in her lap. "Alright, spill. What happened?"

Penny took a deep breath, summoning the strength to recount the disaster of a day she had just endured. She told them about the meeting with Nathan—how her hopes of a full-time job had evaporated, how he had brushed off their previous encounter as if it had meant nothing, and how utterly blindsided she'd felt. Every detail felt like a fresh wound, but with each word, a small sense of relief washed over her. She could trust her friends to understand, to absorb her pain and help her make sense of it.

"Obviously I'm angry. And even if he comes back and tells me the job is mine, his complete disregard for the other night might push me to say no. I didn't expect him to act like meeting me changed his world, but he didn't even acknowledge it."

For a moment, silence hung in the room as her words sank in. Penny could feel Stacie and Mark processing everything she'd just said, their eyes filled with empathy. Stacie, always the nurturer, reached for the pitcher of margaritas on the coffee table and poured out generous glasses for each of them. Handing Penny hers, she offered a small, sad smile.

"Well, I have a silly question," Stacie said, trying to lighten the mood a bit. "Did Mr. Greely actually own the paper? Or does someone else? I'm just wondering who he left it to if he's the owner, and maybe you could talk to them?"

Penny shrugged, swirling her drink absently. "I've never known anyone else to be involved in it, but if I'm being honest, I guess I'm not really sure. Nevertheless, I'm sure the owner is in the family. I can't imagine them going against Nathan."

Mark leaned forward, rubbing his hands together, a gesture he always made when he was gearing up to share something important. "Listen, I know this might not be what you want to hear, but hear me out, okay?"

Mark smiled at her, his eyes kind and thoughtful. Of the three, he was often the most logical, able to see through the fog of emotion to the heart of the matter. His perspective might be exactly what she needed right now.

"Maybe there's another reason why he responded the way he did," Mark suggested, choosing his words carefully. "Maybe he's not exactly single. Plus, with everything going on today was that really the appropriate time to talk about it?"

Penny blinked, taken aback by the possibility. She hadn't even considered that. Maybe Nathan wasn't the heartless jerk she'd painted him to be in her head. After all, he had just lost his uncle, and his life had been turned upside down.

Stacie chimed in, her tone softening. "Mark has a point. We don't know what kind of relationship he had with Mr. Greely, and grief does weird things to people. Maybe today wasn't the best time for him to acknowledge... whatever happened between you."

"I'm not saying he's not a jerk," Mark continued, leaning back in the chair with a sigh. "I'm just saying there might be a deeper reason for his jerkiness."

Penny bit her lip, rolling her glass of margaritas between her hands. "Yeah, I guess I've been too focused on my own feelings. It's not fair to expect him to be perfect right now. But... that doesn't make it any easier, you know?"

Stacie scooted closer, pulling Penny into a side hug. "We get it. But maybe... just maybe, give it time. If he's worth it, he'll figure it out. And if not? You'll be just fine without him."

Penny reached for a handful of chips, savoring the saltiness as she munched them one by one, nodding her head. She felt a small measure of relief at their understanding. "Right now, I'd rather focus on what I do know rather than if Nathan deserves a pass or not," Penny said, waving a hand as if to brush away the earlier tension. She wanted to shift her energy from what she couldn't control to what she could.

Mark grinned, clearly relieved the conversation was shifting. "Now we're talking! Let's figure out what's next for you. Penny 2.0!"

Penny couldn't help but laugh, the sound light and free for the first time all day. "Yeah, alright. Penny 2.0. No more looking back."

Mark shot up from his chair, pacing the room with a burst of energy. "First off, you don't have a contract with the paper, right?"

Stacie gave him a sideways look. "Way to rub salt in the wound, Mark."

Mark held up his hands defensively. "No, no. I'm asking for a reason. If there's no contract, then you own it. The column is yours, and you can do with it whatever you want."

Penny felt a familiar throbbing in her temples, the stress of the situation manifesting as a persistent headache. She massaged the side of her face with her fingers, then got up to retrieve her peppermint oil from the kitchen. As she applied it to her temples, the cool, soothing scent filling her senses, she considered Mark's point.

"I guess so. I mean, Nathan made it pretty clear that I was not under contract with the paper and that my services were no longer needed at this time," she said, trying to keep her frustration in check.

Mark grinned, a spark of inspiration lighting up his face. "And if he didn't make you sign anything, you own all your material. You can use your column to start a podcast, a blog, or a book—whatever you want. The sky's the limit. You need an income. I know it's not the paper, but have you considered working on the radio? I bet they would love your column on the local morning show."

Stacie's eyes darted between Penny and Mark, a puzzled expression on her face. "I thought we were going down the podcast route?"

Penny's heart began to race, a mix of nerves and excitement. Mark was onto something, she realized, and it felt like a light had switched on in her mind. She met Stacie's gaze, nodding eagerly. "We were, and we still could. But podcasts take time to make money, and some never do. But a radio show—I could do that. It doesn't need to be just me sharing. People can call in to a radio show and share their stories just like they can on a podcast. This is a brilliant idea."

"And guess whose uncle happens to work at the radio station?" Mark said, puffing up with pride.

He puffed out his chest, then took a victory lap around Penny's couch while both women cheered him on. Penny's hand moved to her chest, feeling the rapid thump of her heartbeat. This roller coaster of a day was certainly giving her a run for her money. She could see the possibilities stretched out before her like an open road, full of potential and hope.

Penny sat back, a wide smile spreading across her face. "I can't believe I didn't think of it before. I mean, radio makes perfect sense, doesn't it? We could start small, test the waters, and then—who knows?"

Mark nodded, his expression thoughtful. "I think it's the perfect move. You've got the talent and the following. Plus, it's a chance to expand your reach."

Looking around the room, Penny grabbed a stack of notebooks and set them on the coffee table with a thud. "I have all my notes from the columns, even the ones that didn't get published. They'd make great filler material while the show gets up and running." She glanced at Mark, her eyes bright with anticipation. "Mark, how plausible do you think this is? I don't think I can handle losing three jobs in three weeks."

Mark pulled her into a hug, his laughter warm and reassuring. "We won't let you strike out. I'll talk to my uncle tomorrow. He's a great guy. I promise you'll love him."

Penny sat back down, her mind whirring with thoughts as she processed the idea. The radio station was in the next town over, but that wasn't a big deal. She had driven much further while visiting families during her time at Novak. She didn't know much about radio shows, but she couldn't imagine it was that different from writing, right? Surely, she could figure this out.

The three of them sat down and went through the notes, laughing at the memories. Penny couldn't believe some of the crazy dates she had been on. Still, a tinge of worry crept into Penny's mind. She had a treasure trove of material, but her dating life had slowed to a crawl. Her current column had relied heavily on her past romantic misadventures, and she knew that the well would eventually run dry. She needed something new, a fresh angle that would keep listeners engaged. As she turned over the thought in her mind, an idea began to take shape, one that felt both exciting and terrifying.

"Guys," she called out, but the two were deep into her dating failures and didn't hear her at first.

"Guys!" she repeated, more insistently this time. "I have an idea."

Stacie and Mark paused, turning to her with curious

expressions as Penny began pacing the room. Her brain was racing with possibilities, and she could hardly contain the excitement in her voice. Why hadn't she thought of this before? Most towns had an advice column, but they didn't have one on the radio. This was something she could really sink her teeth into.

"What if my radio show was called 'Dear Penny' or… 'A Penny for Your Thoughts'?" She paused, letting the idea hang in the air like a tangible thing.

Stacie's eyes widened with excitement as she caught on. "That's brilliant!" she exclaimed, snapping her fingers and doing a little dance of approval. "The paper doesn't have an advice column, and there's nothing like that on the radio around here. This could really work!"

Mark nodded, his face lighting up with enthusiasm. "And it's something that would translate really well into a podcast. Sorry, I just can't get that possibility out of my head."

Penny's heart raced with exhilaration, feeling as though she was standing on the edge of something big. "No, you're right. It does translate well. I wonder if we could get the radio to support a small podcast, too. They could be recorded simultaneously. Oh my gosh, guys, I'm excited about this. How many ups and downs can one person handle?" She pressed her hands to her face, her cheeks flushed with the thrill of it all. "This isn't a horrible idea."

The three of them dove headfirst into brainstorming, ideas flying across the room with the fervor of a creative storm. They scribbled notes, sketched out potential show formats, and debated segment ideas, each suggestion building on the last. Penny felt buoyed by their support, the fear and uncertainty from earlier in the day melting away in the face of this new adventure.

Mark suggested, "What if we have people call in with their questions or stories? It would make the show interactive and engaging."

Penny nodded, her mind racing. "Yes! And I could share advice based on what I've learned, both from my own experiences and from others. I've got a degree in social work, and I took a few counseling courses. I can use those skills here, just in a different way."

Stacie clapped her hands together. "I love it! You'd be great at this, Penny. People trust you, and you have such a relatable way of presenting things. This could really be something special."

The room was buzzing with ideas, papers scattered across the coffee table as Penny, Stacie, and Mark huddled together. They bounced ideas back and forth like a lively game of ping-pong, filling the space with laughter and bursts of inspiration.

"Okay, so we've got a solid outline for the show," Mark said, leaning back in his chair and tapping his pen against his chin. "What about the presentation itself? We need to make sure we're highlighting why your show will be a hit, and not just for our local audience."

Penny nodded, scribbling down notes in a fresh notebook. "I want to focus on how interactive it will be. People can call in, share their stories, and ask for advice. It's not just me talking; it's a conversation with the community."

Stacie chimed in, her eyes bright with excitement. "And we can include segments that cover trending topics or local events to keep it fresh and relevant. Plus, your column already has a following, so you're not starting from scratch."

Mark nodded approvingly. "Exactly. Uncle Ted loves anything that brings people together, and your show will do just that. It's not just about entertainment—it's about connection."

They continued refining their ideas for another hour, each new thought building on the last until they had a comprehensive plan laid out. Mark took on the role of Penny's coach, preparing her for the meeting with his uncle.

"Remember," he said, his tone both serious and encouraging, "he's quirky and does his own thing, but he's fair. As long as you're genuine and show him the passion you have for this project, he'll see its potential. And I'm his favorite nephew, so you're already in good standing by association."

The idea took off like wildfire. They spent the next couple of hours bouncing ideas around the room, talking through segment ideas, brainstorming show names, and dreaming up ways to make it all work. Mark's excitement was infectious, Stacie's enthusiasm unwavering, and Penny was once again filled with hope.

They eventually helped her tidy up, gathering empty plates and crumpled napkins as they prepared to leave. Penny walked them to the door, feeling a wave of gratitude wash over her.

Mark gave her a big hug, shaking them both back and forth like he was trying to physically shake away any lingering doubts. "I promise to call you as soon as I talk to my uncle. I have a slow morning tomorrow, so I can duck out and introduce the two of you. You've got this."

Stacie blew her a kiss as they headed out into the night, their laughter lingering in the air long after they'd gone. With her house silent once more, Penny took a moment to let the evening's warmth settle in. Even if she was jumping at the next best thing, it was better than having no job at all. And this was a good idea; she could feel it in her bones.

The idea of the radio show filled her with excitement and a sense of purpose that had been missing lately. She turned off the lights in the main part of the house, the soft click of the switch echoing in the quiet space and headed to her bedroom.

After changing into her pajamas, Penny opened her laptop and began researching, "Radio Show 101." As she skimmed through the articles and forums, she couldn't help but chuckle. Anyone looking at her search history might think she was having a midlife crisis. No, she mused, she was just a 30-year-old woman trying to navigate the uncertainty of her life and career.

Feeling more assured about her decision, she realized the key to her success lay in the stories she could tell, the stories that people would share with her. As long as the radio station had someone to handle the technical side of things, she could focus on what she did best, and that was connecting with people through words and ideas.

Her journal sat on the bedside table, beckoning to her. She realized she hadn't written in it for days, nor had she taken time to meditate, and it was showing. She knew she needed to recenter herself, to find that calm amidst the chaos.

Grabbing her palo santo stick, she lit it and let the fragrant smoke cleanse the air around her. The soft glow of candles cast flickering shadows on the walls as she sat cross-legged on her bed, focusing on her breathing. In and out, slow and steady, she let the rhythm wash over her, the tension in her shoulders slowly melting away.

Her grandmother had taught her how to meditate when she was little, insisting that the practice would ground her no matter how turbulent life became. At first, Penny had thought it was silly, but over the years, it had become a vital part of her routine. She could always tell when she'd skipped a few days; the world felt off-kilter, and so did she.

As the minutes passed, Penny felt the craziness of the day lift from her, leaving a sense of peace in its wake. She could almost feel her grandmother's presence beside her, a gentle reminder that she was never truly alone.

Once she felt centered, Penny slipped under the covers, her mind quieter and clearer than it had been in weeks. The sorrow and unease from earlier seemed distant now, replaced by a flicker of optimism. At the end of the day, she was a smart, stubborn, independent woman. She would survive this and come out stronger on the other side.

And as she drifted off to sleep, Penny felt certain that, whatever challenges lay ahead, she was ready to face them head-on. Tomorrow was a new day, and with it came new opportunities. She wasn't sure where the road would lead, but with friends like

Mark and Stacie by her side, she knew she wouldn't be facing it alone.

To be continued...

Review This Book

Your trust in me and your decision to spend your precious time reading this book holds a special place in my heart. Writing is more than a passion for me; it's a deep-seated love that drives me to create captivating stories of hope and rediscovery through later-in-life and second-chance romances. But what truly ignites my soul is the connection I share with readers like you and the invaluable feedback you provide.

If you found the story enjoyable, I would be incredibly grateful if you could spare just a minute to leave a review on Amazon. Your support would mean the world to me, and I genuinely look forward to hearing your thoughts. Your words have the power to uplift and inspire me, and I'm excitedly waiting to learn from your feedback.

Sending you sandy hugs and sunny smiles!

XOXO

Kel Summers

Click here to leave a review on Amazon

Click here to leave a review on BookBub

Click Here to Leave a Review on GoodReads

About Kel Summers

Kel Summers writes clean women's fiction romance books with a focus on later-in-life and second-chance love. Her writing captures the essence of hope, self-discovery, and growth, resonating deeply with readers who appreciate stories of love and new beginnings.

Her personal journey, fueled by her own struggles and heartbreaking loss, led her to leave behind her life in Georgia and venture to the peaceful shores of the Florida Keys. It was there that she found solace, inspiration, and the courage to pursue her lifelong dream of becoming an author.

With her toes in the sand, a pen in her hand, and her faithful and furry canine companion Ivy by her side, she creates tales of love, resilience, and the power of second chances. Through her books, Kel offers readers a chance to escape into beautiful and peaceful coastal settings, where her characters experience personal growth, rekindle lost passions, and find love when they least expect it.

Kel Summers's books resonate with readers seeking heartwarming stories that transport them to the beach, where love and new beginnings flourish. Her clean and uplifting romances capture the beauty of later-in-life love and the profound impact it can have on one's life. With each new release, Kel continues to captivate readers and remind them that, no matter the challenges faced, there is always an opportunity for healing and a second chance at finding true happiness.

Discover the healing power of second chances and the magic of love in Kel Summers' later-in-life, women's fiction, clean beach romances.

Click here for a complete list of books by Kel Summers or visit https://linktr.ee/kelsummers

Made in United States
North Haven, CT
13 July 2025

70649992R00065